# *They Was Holdin' Hands*

A Novel By

*Venera Di Bella Barles*

Venera
Let's enjoy this journey together —
[illegible]

Venera Di Bella Barles

# *They Was Holdin' Hands*

A Novel by

## *Venera Di Bella Barles*



ISBN: 1-59507-065-6

**ArcheBooks Publishing Incorporated**

www.archebooks.com

9101 W. Sahara Ave.
Suite 105-112
Las Vegas, NV 89117



This book is entirely a work of fiction. The names, characters, places, and incidents depicted herein are either products of the author's imagination or are used fictitiously. Any resemblance to actual events or locales or persons, living or dead, is entirely coincidental.

Hardcover First Edition: 2005

ArcheBooks Publishing

# *Dedication*

FOR

MY INAMORATA

EDWARD THE GOOD

THANK YOU FOR YOUR

LOVE AND LOYALTY

# *Table of Contents*

*Forgotten? No, we never do forget:*
*We let the years go by; wash them clean with tears,*
*Leave them to bleach out in the open day,*
*Or lock them careful by, like dead friends' clothes,*
*Till we shall dare unfold them without pain—*
*But we forget not, never can forget.*

**Dinah Mulock Craik** (1826-1887)
From: "A Flower of a Day,"

# Chapter 1
# The Hermits

The question nagged at me—why did it end this way?

It was January, 1987. I was waiting in the Seattle airport terminal to board a plane to visit my daughter in Maryland when I glanced at the seat next to me where someone had left a copy of that day's *Seattle Times.* I spotted an article that stunned me.

•

> Three elderly sisters were found dead yesterday near the small mining community of Pine Grove Haven, PA. The reclusive women were discovered huddled together around a wood-burning stove in the kitchen of their rural farmhouse. "It looks like suicide," a sheriff's department spokesman said. The spinster sisters, Violet, ninety-two, Daisy, eighty-eight and Rose

> Hinkle, eighty-three, were discovered after a neighbor arrived to shovel their driveway and noticed newspapers had piled up for nearly a week. Autopsy results are expected to confirm death by exposure...

•

Something about this news piece pulled at me. The notion of the women dying in such a lonely fashion sent shivers up my spine. As I read the whole article, noting the names and ages of the women, the question kept demanding an answer—*why?*

Perhaps it bothered me because I was facing my sixty-fifth birthday and could taste my own mortality.

Perhaps it was because I'd fought my own battles with depression and thoughts of suicide and won.

In my early years, I struggled with hopelessness that left me emotionally naked. I was sucked of energy battling my parents that brought their fractured childhood into their parenting skills. A heavy-handed father who scrambled his family's psyche because of his own needs. A mother, who bowed out of life because it was safer.

I married my friend at nineteen, but was angry because I couldn't grow old with him—I lost the battle to keep him healthy. It was much like the struggle to keep our marriage alive. It was only towards our later years did he understand the word *intimacy.*

To keep my personal problems at bay I had always used a heavy schedule. In my early years, after the birth of my children, I fought depression and thoughts of suicide. I endured post-partum depression so noxious it stole from my own babies and husband. The unexpected death of a baby son left me with no energy to grieve. Therapy helped dramatically, but I continued to fight depression until my late forties. In my fifties, I had gathered most of the answers, but I needed to learn how to incorporate them into my life.

A few years ago, as I wrote my memoir, I was right back on the emotional battleground again as I opened the box of twin demons—depression and suicidal tendencies. This time I won because the written word helped to conquer the inner beast that threatened to snatch control.

But these three sisters' suicides, if it was that, at their advanced ages, made me feel vulnerable, raising an uncomfortable troubled patter in my body. Now, once again, I had come to a crossroads, asking, *what was that all about?*

I tucked the paper into my purse, wondering which of the three Hinkle spinsters made the decision for them to die that critical day. Was it ninety-two-year-old Violet, the oldest, or was it Daisy, eighty-eight, or perhaps eighty-three-year-old Rose? I wanted to know why they chose to die this way. What happens after we live a long lifetime? Do we come to an agreement with our attitudes? Thoughts and questions swam through my brain.

What could I learn or recognize, with reference to myself, by looking into the lives of these three aged women? How different were we?

The incident stuck in my head all through my visit with my daughter in Maryland and for a year afterward. During that time, a need to understand made me find out all I could—I contacted the local paper for a more in-depth report, even called the town's sheriff's office trying to find answers that would help me comprehend what had happened. The deputy's voice grew cool as I stumbled over the fact that I wasn't a relative and had no real connection to the women. I realized people were bound to think my interest abnormal.

To make my questions seem more natural, I decided it was time to really investigate what happened and gather material to write a book about them. Then I would have a legitimate reason to give for my curiosity—even if deep down I knew my motives were more complex and too tangled to fully define, even to myself.

Most of my early writing was magazine articles, except for my memoir. This would be my first novel. Somehow, when I write, I feel heard.

A year later, I flew east again. Born and raised in upper New York State, I had an idea of what I might encounter in Pennsylvania in January.

Arriving shortly before noon, I rented a car at the Baltimore airport, tried the heater, and made sure I had chains in the trunk. It was a lonely drive, and I definitely didn't want to get stuck. An old tune on the radio took me back to the many road trips I had taken with my late husband--the silly banter of marriage. I had decided to remain uninvolved and single, but a trip like this reminded me of how much I missed his company.

Just outside the central coal-mining community of Pine Grove Haven, in a remote holler, was the stark setting in which the Hinkle sisters had spent their entire lives. I assumed that the people here were poles apart from where I now lived in the Pacific Northwest. But how were they different?

I sensed I had entered a society of privacy as I drove along the dirt roads lined with leafless trees. The night before, the temperature had dropped to five below.

Early in the afternoon, I stopped at a convenience store and gas station to ask a young mechanic for directions. I showed him my map and asked if he knew Carl Fenster, and if he knew how to get to the man's house.

"Yep!" he replied, as his warm breath hit the freeze. "I know Carl." It was awkward for him to simultaneously talk, smoke, and wipe his greasy hands with a rag. "Can't imagine what business you'd have with him."

I smiled politely, avoiding his question. He pointed out the directions and then watched me as I got back into the car. On my way, I first stopped to look at the two-story, dilapidated Hinkle farmhouse, nestled near the bottom of a ravine. As I drove down the long, steep, frozen dirt lane, a feeling of solitude came over me. Could I live this way, I wondered, so far from civilization...so seemingly simple?

But was it as simple as it appeared? Were they really afraid?

*"Don't be afraid, Carmela—if you are good, the bogeyman won't get you. Remember what happened to that little girl that died."*

*"Don't say that, Mommy. I don't want to go into a box."*

I shook off the unpleasant memory. I preferred to focus on the here and now, rather than dwell on my less than perfect childhood.

I drew my coat tighter against the cold and looked over the scene. My God, it was bleak out here. I wondered what inner darkness drove these women. How did one get used to this isolation?

Getting back into my car, I shifted the car into gear and returned to the main highway and backtracked to find Fenster's time worn farmhouse, nestled in a treed patch near a creek. Nearby, his rusty plow and faded red tractor sat dormant in the icy, gray fields. On a sagging clothesline attached to the side of the house worn towels hung alongside overalls frozen into alien shapes. I drove nearer and parked.

I stood gazing at the paint-starved wooden door before I knocked. Carl Fenster answered. I introduced myself and refreshed his memory of why I was there.

"Oh, yeah. I been wonderin' if you'd come. I got your letter." He stood in the doorway, one hand on the upper frame. His lips disappeared. "Seems like a long way to come just to ask questions. What you got in mind?"

He studied me as I told him what I would like to get from my visit.

His voice was loud and unwavering. "Hell, them reporters were swarmin' all over this valley last year when them girls died. Comin' out of every damn crack. All you gotta do is read those newspapers."

I pulled back. I felt like a peacock, all my bright colors against the drabness of my surroundings. I didn't get the sense that he would invite me in.

"So, what makes you think we have anything here that's spicy for a book? Always somebody tryin' to make a buck off a somebody else's business."

I told him I understood how it must feel to have people prying into personal matters. I disclosed that I felt a sense of embarrassment when it came to anyone finding out distressing things about my family. I stopped short of telling him that my father physically abused my mother, sister, and me.

He didn't speak for a moment. "*Humph.* Misfortunes ain't somethin' we like to talk about. So much happenin' all the time. We wouldn't have much else to flap about. And that one over there in the holler's had us all bowled over. Nobody saw it comin'."

I assured him that I would certainly try not to misuse anything that I heard.

"Well, I guess you can c'mon in. Did you hear? C'mon in."

He held the door open, staring at me as I entered, motioning to a straight chair by a table. "Sit yerself down, right here."

Fenster, a robust man, removed his worn parka from a chair and hung it on a nail behind the door. His stern voice filled the room, "They was funny ole girls." He groused as he moved about the dismal kitchen, "Not used to havin' folks in here. My Dora knew how to make people feel easy. She knew just the right thing to say to calm me. You remind me a little of her. Let me stick another piece of wood in the firebox."

I appreciated his efforts to relax and reach out. He continued to ask me about my family and my writing career.

"Your pa and ma are dead? Italian immigrants you say?"

I nodded.

"You know, a lot of miners here were Italian. Stuck together, but hard workers. I had me a good friend, Salvatore. He died." He turned to observe how I reacted. I told him coincidentally my father's name was Salvatore. His eyebrows knit together. "Got some coffee on the stove. Like me to pour you a cup?"

He took off his baseball cap, ran his gnarled hand through his grizzled hair, and then replaced the hat.

"I just finished plowin' their road. I usually plowed it if it had more'n a coupla inches of snow. They didn't take the car out much anymore, but I knew between the three of them they could get to the mailbox, even though they was in poor health. Violet, she was in her nineties, was pretty crippled up with arthritis. Daisy broke her hip awhile back. Didn't mend that good. Folks took turns bringin' them food."

I watched Fenster's large, weathered hands as he poured two cups of steaming black coffee.

"Where did you say you was from? Seattle? I never been there. I never been out of this valley. Grew up here. So did the Hinkle sisters. In those days we did our shoppin' from the *Montgomery Ward* and *Sears & Roebuck* catalog. My father came fer work from the Kentucky mines. Met my Dora here."

Fenster didn't speak for a few minutes as he stuffed tobacco into his handmade pipe. He lit the bowl and drew in deeply.

"Lost my wife a coupla of years ago. Sick as the divil. Two weeks and she were gone. My three kids left some time back, to make their way someplace better."

I told him how sorry I was for the loss of his wife. His eyes revealed his sorrow. The kitchen still reflected the touches of Dora's life. Amidst the baking bowls, sacks of flour and faded curtains were four well-used cast-iron pans—a large stew pot, a medium fryer, a deep one for the fire, and a multi-purpose.

A black Labrador, which Fenster called 'Satin', plodded into the kitchen, sniffed my hand, made three turns and with a few groans, lay down close to the stove on a small rug. I asked Fenster about his children.

Still careful, he proceeded to answer the questions. "Well, my daughter and her husband seem to being doin' fine. She cain't have kids. She don't like that much." He took a long draw on his pipe and watched the smoke swirl upwards. "Yep! My oldest boy is a fireman in Harrisburg. He wants me to sell and git out of here. But he don't understand, this is my home. My youngest son, Merle, he lives in Minneapolis now. Can't predict what he's up to. Unsteady. Comes out here to see me a few times a year. The only one that can't settle down. Been married a coupla times, but can't seem to stick with that neither."

He avoided looking at my face. I could hear the heartache of a father who feels powerless. I caught a narrowing of his eyes as if he were searching to see if he had said too much. I didn't pursue the discussion of his son. I changed the subject and asked Carl to describe what he found at the Hinkle house.

"Well, hell! They was probably dead five or six days." Fenster was nervous and fidgeted with his pipe. "I guess it was a Tuesday when Selma, down the road, called and said the mail was pilin' up in the mailbox 'till the door on it wouldn't shut. People were busy with the holidays and weren't paying as much mind to the girls. They said they had everything they needed for a spell. The Hinkles was odd folks. They couldn't see any of our houses up here over the ridge from the bottom of their ravine. At first I thought it happened durin' the day—'cause the lights weren't on, but then we found out they stopped paying their light bill. Fenster rose from the rough-made chair. "Wouldn't nar matter anyways. They was the kind of people who'd sit in the dark."

He stopped and looked at me writing down the information. He folded his arms firmly across his chest.

"What'd you say you was gonna do with all this account? *Huh*. Writin' a book?"

Once more I confirmed that I was considering the idea. I explained how the story affected me and how it was pushing me to understand people's motives. I asked permission to visit the home and spend some time looking things over. I felt his eyes stealing into my head as I asked more questions and made my notes.

"Well, them sisters was a tough team, just like their pa. You couldn't put anythin' over on them. No sir. No sir. They was all smart. Why, little ole Daisy, the middle of the three, used to write every day in little books. Don't know what she wrote, but for as long as I knew her, she liked to write. Now, if I let you go into that house, I don't want you upsettin' or takin' anythin', you hear?"

He stopped talking and bent to rub the dog's prone body. Satin moaned deeply.

"You know, it was eleven degrees in that house. They must have been dead for a week or so. I aimed my flashlight into the kitchen, saw all three of them girls on the kitchen floor—all huddled together—one layin' down, two sittin' up. Two had their feet pushed under the wood stove. They must have stuck everythin' they owned on their backs. They had on layers of jackets, sweaters, and blankets."

Fenster breathed heavily. "Rose looked like she was talkin' to Daisy. Her eyes were kinda open. I knew them girls most of my life. It kilt me to see them there like that. I don't know what got into them. Never saw it comin'."

The hair rose on my arms and the back of my neck.

"Like I sez, they was holdin' hands."

# *Excerpts from the Diaries of Miss Daisy Maude Hinkle*

## 1917—June 11th

Today is my sixteenth birthday. I don't expect Ma will say anything nice to me. None of us girls ever get a birthday gift or anything that says they are glad we were born. I saw a nice piece of material down at the company store. It had pretty blue and yellow flowers. Ma says that's too frivolous. My friend, Marlee Lou's mother and father are so kind to their family. Even though they are poor and needy they are always smiling. Marlee Lou got her grandmother's cameo brooch when she turned sixteen.

Violet and I are always knitting sweaters for the miners children—I help her rip out old sweaters we collect and we make the new ones all different colors. The children love them.

**They Was Holdin' Hands**

We are at war. Not sure what that means. Our life couldn't get any worse. I wonder what my life will be, as I get older. It doesn't look as if Pa will ever leave these coalmines. I wonder if it's worse to die in a coalhole, or in war?

# Chapter 2
# Cautious Sociability

On the main highway, a few miles north of Pine Grove Haven's sign, I found a motel with a small coffee shop, *Etta Mae's Drift On Inn Motel and Diner*. I rented a room for a week. Etta Mae Jackson, the proprietor, was a tall, no-nonsense straight-standing black woman, built like the *Michelin Man*. She was one sharp cookie, even without showing any evidence of a formal education.

Etta Mae took the suitcases out of the trunk of my rental car and hauled them like a stevedore up to my room.

"Them's clean towels in there. Everthin's clean. Extra blanket an' pillow in the closet. If'n ya need anythin', come up front! I make a good breakfast. It'll stick to your innards. I got stuffed pork chops for supper tonight. Now, keep your door locked."

I thanked her and told her I would be in for dinner. She

departed, leaving behind an aroma of fried food.

The place reminded me of the 50's. A small black-and-white TV sat on the edge of the bureau next to a county phone book and a *Gideon.* It was the type of motel that had low wattage light bulbs. It was minimally furnished but clean.

I took off the heavy, wool pea jacket that I'd bought when one of my daughters worked at an Army and Navy surplus. After I tucked my clothes into the small chest of drawers, I glanced at my image in the mirror. What was I doing? These people weren't anything like me. We had nothing in common.

I smoothed my graying auburn hair, adjusted my hoop earrings, and reapplied sable-colored shadow to my eyelids. After all, I came from a different culture. And, my goodness, healthwise I was in very good condition: I played tennis two times a week, did my own housekeeping and gardening, wrote intensely, went to the theater with friends, and volunteered in the community as much as I possibly could. I was fashionable and wore my near sixty-five years splendidly. Not bad for an old broad.

On Sunday, I attended services at Pine Grove Haven Church of God, a white building with a tall steeple near the broken-down remains of the company store. Carl Fenster introduced me to a few of the locals. He explained who I was and why I had come to Pine Grove Haven. I appreciated his asking each of the parishioners to be "helpful and honest" with information. Carl appeared to be a favorite and respected elder. We stood together outside the church after the service. One by one, I met the reticent, but polite, parishioners.

Selma Webster greeted me first, a pleasing widow in her seventies, of medium height, thick in the middle, with a full bosom, and a double chin. She said she was helping raise her three granddaughters.

Carl jingled the coins in his pocket. "Now this here's Selma. She's a good gal. Selma, this here's Miz Carmela Valente. I told her maybe you could take her on over to the Hinkle farm? She wants to take a look and make some notes."

Thomas Maas, a bachelor, who lived with his elderly mother Elsa, lit a cigarette the moment he stepped out of the church. He was hesitant when Fenster approached him. They talked quietly for a few moments, and then they walked toward me.

"Tom, I want you to meet this lady. Carmela Valente." He turned to me. "Am I sayin' yer name right?"

I nodded. At first Thomas Maas stood still.

"She's trying to understand what happened to them Hinkle girls last year," Carl said, "I told her she could visit the house."

Thomas raised his hand in a gesture that seemed half a salute and half a way to avoid shaking my hand.

"You sure came a rotten time of year. Didn'tcha read the newspapers about them? All over the news. There was enough muck raked up at that time," he said with a lisp.

I acknowledged I did, startled at his defensiveness. I tried to explain that I wasn't necessarily investigating the deaths but hoping to know them on a personal level.

"*Phah!* Why would that matter to you? They're strangers. And besides what good would it do them girls now?"

I agreed, but added that gaining knowledge about others helps us to understand ourselves. I asked if he wasn't of the same mind.

He softened. His hand went to his face as he spoke, lest I see a mouth of missing teeth. "Well, certainly, I understand that. Sorry, but I can't help being suspicious of the ways of people." He extended his hand to shake mine.

At that point the Schoen family came over to us and stood

by quietly—John, Martha, their two grandchildren, and John's brother, Albert. In a few minutes I saw the bald, red-faced preacher walk toward the small assemblage. Reverend Cyrus Miller was a large, paunchy man in his sixties. I was told he had been pastor for many years at the church. Walking by his side was his dour-looking, angular wife, Nell.

"Did I hear that yer gonna stay for a week, Miz Valente?" Pastor Miller asked with a large, ingratiating smile.

I was surprised he already knew my name. He reminded me of an old-time character actor, still on stage, whose name escaped me.

"Now, when you go back into the church, we have a table set up for coffee and sweets. Help yerself to Martha Schoen's ginger cakes. There's plenty there, now, so don't go skimpin'. Martha's a good woman, always makes extra."

He didn't wait for my reply, but barged ahead with his own train of thought.

"Miz Valente, did I hear right? Carl told me you're a grandmother? Widow? Seems like the family would worry about you being gone so long and so far away. Can't see what you could find appealin' in these hills." He shook his head. "I understand Selma might take you on over to the Hinkle house tomorrow to have a look around."

It was obvious news traveled fast in this isolated community. Selma had just agreed to take me a few minutes before.

"It's been shut for near a year. Awful shame. Them girls was shut up like hermits. Pretty talkative an' contrary at times when they was younger. Then it was like someone flipped a switch. Them sisters had health problems in recent years."

Everyone eyed me. Their faces tightened up as the preacher revealed information. Their closed arms protected their secrets. My own skills were being tested as I did my best to present a non-threatening aspect tó these folks. Would they understand my interest, prying into their private thoughts, thoughts they had already sorted?

I felt a sadness in this valley, written in its history of times when the coalminers went to work in deep, dark mines. I remembered what Carl Fenster told me, how the miners would leave for work early and return late at night, so weary that they could hardly address their family's needs. Men worked in the subterranean guts of the earth in near total darkness. They mined coal mostly by hand, shoveled each piece into a small rail car, and pushed it down the gangway to the shaft where it was hoisted to the surface in a one-ton bucket. Generations of sons, fathers, and grandfathers mined coal in the anthracite seam in Schuylkill County, one of many throughout Pennsylvania and other states. They entered as boys and came out as old men.

Only one color prevailed—black. Hair? Black. Faces? Black. Bodies and clothing? Black. Lungs? Black. Death lived easily in these vales.

I asked Maas, clean-shaven and never without a cigarette, about his days in the mine. He looked older than the sixty-plus years he said was his age.

"Humph. There's nothin' to tell. There's nothin' but sorrow down there," he said, short of breath and fighting back tears from slate blue eyes in sunken sockets. "You leave part of yerself down there. Lost my pa, three brothers, an uncle, and many a friend."

He looked uncomfortable. We stood silent for quite some time, and then I asked Thomas if he knew the Hinkle family. A line from that first newspaper article flashed in and out of my brain: *"It looks like suicide," a sheriff's department spokesman said.*

Thomas glanced at Carl Fenster and nodded. "Yup. Mostly

before my time—I'm a couple a years older than the Hinkle's youngest girl, Lily, and she were a lot younger than the rest of 'em. Old man Hinkle worked the mines since he was a small stone. He was tough on his missus. Awful tough. Tough on the girls, too. Hmm. I remember my ma tellin' how they lost Zachary, their son. They was hoistin' the bucket up and the damn thing broke. Come smashin' right down on him."

In between his hacking, Maas took quick, short puffs on a hand-rolled cigarette. He attempted to straighten his consumptive frame.

"When we was young fellers, Albert Schoen an' me tried to date Lily. Albert even wanted to marry her, but her father didn't much like that idear. Remember that, Carl? An' my ma sure didn't want me thinkin' about women. I gave it up as a bad idear."

Carl smiled and rubbed his nose.

Thomas watched me and continued, "Them Hinkle girls knew they would have to take care of things after their parents bit the dust. An' they did fine for quite awhile. Even worked in a garment factory. Violet, the oldest girl, she were the most active. She were the one that drove the others around. Lily left an' made her own way. Daisy, when she weren't fightin' for the unions, always had her nose in a book. Then ole Rose used to teach the folks, mostly boys and fellers how to read. But she started gettin' muddy brained."

Carl added, "She never did get over losing Zack, her twin, but I think something else was goin' on in her head and it got worse as she got older. Lotta times, you'd ask her a question, but she just stayed on course, never answerin' anythin'."

By now I had a circle of listeners about me, but few offered any observations.

I asked why he thought things turned out as they did with

the Hinkle women.

"Now, that's one to figure out. Maybe, they was tired," Carl answered.

I grew cold standing in one place. I'd forgotten the depth of discomfort of eastern wintry weather.

Thomas continued, his eyes darting around, "Daisy tole me that when they was young girls, they helped their ma on the farm. Isn't that right, Carl? They made butter, growed the vegetables, and milked the cows. Their pa, Sam, worked the early shift in the mines. Then when he finished there, he picked up the farm goods and went on his market route to neighbor communities. After he died, they did all the farmin' and chores. We all have to adjust quick when someone drops out."

Selma interrupted Maas, "Yep. And Daisy said one time how they all dropped out of school at an early age, except Lily. She went on to high school. The other girls did their studyin' at home. They didn't none of them marry. Well, I should say except for Lily, she married and moved to Pittsburgh after Albert married Amy Bronson. Lily didn't come back too often after that. She were different."

Maas smoked to the end of the wrapped cigarette until it became one with his stained fingers.

"Did I tell you Rose used to teach older folks how to read and write?" Carl asked. "She were the brainy type. Well, they was all brainy. Lucille, their mother, always made sure they had books, and she made sure they learnt."

During the discussion, they seemed to focus on something in the distance, but never on me. A man with cold, ferret-like eyes stood by the door of the church. The ruggedly handsome man, powerfully built, had gray-streaked jet-black hair worn to his shoulders. He stood in the background staring intently at me as Maas and I conversed. I watched the smoke from his cigarette encircle his face like a veil. He wore a well-used aviator's brown leather jacket over denim pants and shirt. The whole enhanced his manly vigor.

Maas saw my reaction to the man. "Don't pay no mind to Clive Mooney, he's an odd sort. He don't like to talk much, but likes the ladies. Works for the brewery. Delivers barrels 'round the counties. Lives down a piece from the Schoen place in a shack near the crick. Does fill-in small jobs, handyman type. Has done that for years. His paw, Calvin, used to do the same when he was alive."

Finally, I was introduced to Albert Schoen, a straight, tall, handsome, and strongly built gentleman with a shock of white, wavy hair. I saw a gentle refinement in his manner. He appeared to be in his early sixties, well groomed with a faint scent of *4711* toilet water. His clothes were modest, but better than the rest of the group. Under his heavy jacket, his shirt was buttoned tight at his thick neck. His steel-gray eyes seemed to pierce my thoughts.

"How do you do, Ms. Valente. Carl Fenster was telling me about you. I hope your accommodations at Etta Mae's are worthy."

I was intrigued by his slow modulated speech pattern.

"We don't have much, but what we have is decent and unadulterated. Carl tells me you're researching the Hinkle family. You're a writer, I understand. Anything in particular you're looking for?"

I confessed to him that I still didn't know what it was I wanted, but I hoped I would know in a day or two. I asked him if he felt the deaths were accidental.

"Interesting question," he stepped back and dug his shoe into the frozen earth, his hands jammed into his pockets, shoulders arched. "We were deeply shocked by their deaths. It's hard to say. To my mind the scene seemed fairly staged. They did have friends and neighbors. I know they could have had help. But they had become reclusive. Many times these hills shelter attitudes."

Yes, interesting, I thought. I was surprised at the depth of his answers. Lives are forever layered. Certainly, I knew mine was. I asked if he lived in the area or was he just visiting.

"At the present I live with my brother, John, and his family on Black Creek Road," he said. "I would be glad to help if you need."

I thanked him for his generous offer. A pleasant, moon-faced woman came and stood by his side.

"This is my sister-in-law, Martha," he announced.

With her eyes cast down, Martha, who had seen middle age, took my hand limply. "Pleased to meetcha, Miz."

I complimented her on the ginger cakes, which I'd had with coffee when Selma took me inside for a few moments.

"Thank you. I'm glad you like them. Now, I kin set another plate if you'd like to c'mon over for supper. I'm makin' *blind pigeons*. We usually has that on Sundays. "

I smiled warily.

Albert laughed and said, "Oh that's stuffed cabbage. Don't they sometimes call it *halupkies,* Martha?"

Martha nodded her tightly permed head. "My ma used to call it that."

"You're probably not familiar with the local slang, some call it *coal-speak*. This place is rich with the heritage of many ethnicities."

I was amazed at the different levels of education in this small mining community. What were these folks all about? My prejudices expected them to lack culture with all this scarcity surrounding them. I thought I had everything sorted out, yet the more they said to me, the more their wisdom canceled my predictions. Certainly there was no ignorance here, except for mine.

I accepted Martha's offer.

•

For each evening, I was invited to dinner by a different family. I counted myself lucky. Within days, I might establish myself in the close community and conversations might not seem as guarded.

Back in my motel room, I tested my memory to better remember all of them. I jotted down the new names and facts I had garnered. Carl Fenster living alone with Satin, his black lab, and had his children scattered about. I felt sad about the solitude since his wife Dora had died. Then there was Thomas Maas, the bachelor living with his mother, Elsa. The Schoens were an interesting family. Two very different brothers, John and Albert—one married to Martha, with a grown son and two grandchildren, the other appeared more educated.

Would they understand, or would I insult them by bringing them the small gifts, minor tokens of gratitude for their hospitality? I wrapped two tea towels in tissue paper and headed for the Schoen house on Black Creek Road. Questions came as I drove the narrow two-lane road. I wondered how each of the inhabitants crossed Violet, Daisy, and Rose Hinkle's paths. What were the hatreds, secrets, love matches? How did they share in their tragedies? What were their strengths?

For years I'd been fascinated by people's lives and their environment and how they were different from mine. I read true-crime books to understand what makes offenders suddenly go off the deep end. I wanted to know it all.

As I drove out to join the Schoen's for dinner, I felt nervous. The modest Schoen house came into view. It was a pale yellow saltbox with white trim. Frozen furrowed rows looked ready for spring planting. The garden looked tended even though it was the dead of winter. The limbs of large scarlet oaks stripped-bare seemed to protect the homestead and an ice-edged, swiftly moving creek ran behind the property.

I expected gloom but was taken aback by the brightness that greeted me as I entered.

"Sit right in there, Miz Valente," said John, Albert's younger brother, as he welcomed me to his home. He pointed me in the direction of the parlor and the davenport with crocheted doilies. Although he lacked the style of his older brother, he was nonetheless tall, ruddy, and good-looking. I could tell John knew manual labor intimately by his slightly stooped back and rough hands.

Martha came out of her kitchen wearing a flowered cobbler apron over her lace-collared church dress. I greeted her and handed her the tea towels.

Her face reddened as she opened the tissue. "Well, my goodness, Miz, you didn't have to do this. But they are lovely. Did you bring your appetite for the stuffed cabbage and apple crisp?"

I told her how much I appreciated her invitation. The smells of her home were reminiscent of my childhood in my grandmother's house. A warmth I had forgotten.

Martha squeezed my hand, and then called to her grandson to wash up and come to supper, and to bring down a chair from her sewing machine."

Albert escorted me to the small dining area, where a girl

with long braids had put a bowl of biscuits on the thin white tablecloth. She shyly backed away without looking at me. I smiled at her and Albert pushed the Windsor seat in for me. The boy brought the chair to the table and settled down, as did the men. Martha took the seat across from me. Her granddaughter sat next to her older brother.

"These are our two grandchildren. Our son is a long-haul trucker and his wife drives with him. The kids stay with us when they're on the road. Julian is eleven, and Isabella, she's gonna be eight."

Each child raised his hand in a general salute. Their grandfather made a slight sound and all bowed their heads for a moment of prayer. I remembered my father making the sign of the cross before our meals—meals that typically ended with anger and harsh words. The lip homage of religion had little meaning to me.

The overhead fixture bathed the room in light. I could still see the remains of dusk outside the lace-curtained windows. A potted "mother-in-law's tongue," with its long, spiked fronds stood tall on a metal stand, and on a small painted table African violets colored the area. I complimented Martha on the pleasant surroundings. She thanked me timidly. She was a bit younger than her husband.

"Albert, can you pass the potatoes to Miz Valente?" said Martha.

A silence came over the family as dishes moved around the table. John began to eat, the others followed. The food was flavorful and abundant.

At last, John spoke up, "What did you have in mind to find out? We're not used to outsiders askin' a lot of questions. Everyone has so many misfortunes that nobody likes to complain."

Once again, I explained the reasons for my visit to the valley. His defensive approach softened as he accepted my response.

"Well, I kin tell you that Carl Fenster plowed the Hinkle fields for the last twenty years. Grew grain on their acres, most of it not too usable. Paid them Hinkle girls about nine-hundred dollars a year for the privilege. Tough to make a livin' sellin' grain. Hard country to stay ahead of."

I told him how much I valued his input. I said I realized how hard it must be to live in such a tough area, where there is so much sorrow. I shared how much my father disliked talking about his family's poverty and sadness. He wouldn't admit to anyone that he couldn't make it here in the United States.

John shook his head back and forth. "Well then, you know what we're talkin' about. It's everywhere."

I asked Albert if he worked the mines or fields.

He hesitated and then replied in a soft, slow tone, as if it was an effort, "When I was younger I did, Ms. Valente. Right here with my father." He sipped his coffee, and looked beyond me out the window at the moon shining on the creek. "But then I worked for many years in New York City as an architect."

I straightened in my chair. I had guessed there was something different about this man. I wondered why he had returned. There truly were many layers of stories. His strong, assured manner suddenly appeared restrained.

Albert stood up and asked, "Ms. Valente, would you care for some more coffee or another serving of Martha's wonderful apple crisp?"

I declined the extra dessert.

His hand shook as he poured my coffee. "John and I were born in this house. Later I moved to that bungalow down by the creek, also owned by our family." He pointed to the barely visible one-story clapboard. "I lived there until I was thirty. It was after..."

Suddenly, Martha interrupted Albert as if she didn't want him to continue. "Now, Julian, you help Isabella clear the table and get on up to do your homework." She turned back to me. "I understand, Miz Valente, that you're going to the Hinkle house tomorrow with Selma Webster. She knew the family well."

Albert remained standing, cup in hand. He watched us as Martha continued, "Selma Webster, you met her today at church, worked for awhile, when she was young, with Violet, Daisy and Rose in the garment factory." Martha moved closer to me. "Now, Samuel, their father, died in a mine explosion back in '43. Suffocated from carbon monoxide gas, you know. In his sixties, I believe. That explosion took a lotta lives. Hard to keep up with all the calamities in this valley."

Martha looked at me to check how I was receiving her information, then went on, "I'll tell you who else understands things pretty good and that's Fannie from the garage on the main highway. She seems to know how people think. A little hard around the edges, but her heart is bigger than her skin. She's had plenty of her own miserable times.

"But getting on back to the Hinkles," Martha turned to her brother-in-law, "Albert, didn't Rose teach you and John?"

"She did, Martha."

John jumped into the conversation, "Rose Hinkle used to go house to house in the evening to help with lessons for us boys who had to work the mines. Sometimes we'd go to her place. She taught me to read n' write. She'd find ways of gettin' used books from other counties. Nice lady. She was quieter and more self-conscious than her other sisters. Ole Elsa Maas says they was good-lookin' women when they was young. Rose even helped our pa with his English. He come over from Germany a teen-boy. Couldn't speak a word of English. But by God, he managed, even though he never shook the thick accent."

I told them of my own father having to learn the language and about the employment discrimination, which faced foreigners. Every ethnic group took their turn at being gored with prejudice.

Albert replied, "Yes, there was plenty of that. We had many Italians working here, as a matter of fact. Many nationalities and races worked these mines. They tended to be clannish. Safety in numbers, I guess."

Martha and the Schoen brothers seemed to enjoy the after-dinner chat and giving surface profiles of the townsfolk. Martha recalled the strict Hinkle father and dutiful mother. "Mr. Hinkle ruled the roost. Not much got by him. People said he never got over it after Zachary, their son, died. Of course, Zackary died before I was borned. I'm almost of an age with Lily—she was a couple of years above me in school. She were a lot younger than the other girls."

John sat quietly for a while and then remarked. "All of us lost so many of our kin to those holes in the ground. But the women worked pretty hard above, didn't they, Martha?"

Martha shook her curly head from side to side. "There ain't no way to measure the pain of it all."

I could see there was much to learn from the inhabitants of Pine Grove Haven. I felt easier about visiting the Hinkle farmhouse in the hollow.

Martha advised, "Better to dress warm tomorrow, Miz. The electricity is off in the Hinkle house. They say the temperature is droppin' agin' tonight."

# *Excerpts from the Diaries of Miss Daisy Maude Hinkle*

**1917—July**

Ma says we'd better learn all we can because life is not going to be easy. Ma says that I should be working and studying instead of spending my time writing in my diary. She says I have uppity ways. I feel so sad when she says things like that. I help the family all the time, but she is always bitter and says unkind things to us girls.

Pa doesn't want Violet and me to talk to boys.

Rose and Zachary, the twins, are thirteen now and Pa has been taking Zachary into the mines to work with him. The twins are very close. Pa seems to favor Rose.

•

**1920—December 31st**

Oh what a disastrous and wretched day! My life will never be the same without my sweet brother, Zachary. The mines have killed him. He was crushed beyond recognition. How will I live without him?

We barely had enough money to bury him properly. I hate this place. What a way to always remember New Year's Eve! If there is a God he is not looking at this part of the world.

•

**1922—March**

We have to break this cycle of assaults and rapes. I visited Rosetta Lunetta today. She looks terribly down in the dumps. She prepares food for the paymaster and his guards and every time her husband is working down in the hole, Paymaster McParlan comes around and bothers her. She said to me she feels helpless with her three little children. Rosetta hasn't said anything to Pepino. I know he would murder McParlan.

After all these years, Ma is going to have a baby again.

It's been two years since Zachary died. He and his twin, Rose, were inseparable. She is still so sad – she said, "It's as if one of my limbs has been cut off. Zachary used to protect me when Pa came around."

Rose seems ailing lately she must have an intestinal thing. Can't hold anything down.

# *Chapter 3*
# *Sanctuary*

My hands perspired on the steering wheel as I neared the Hinkle house. I wasn't sure what I would feel once I went into the place. The drab, once-white paint indicated the drain of life. Barren trees framing the two-story saltbox looked like wires darting out of the roof. Selma was waiting for me in her faded red Ford Ranchero. I noticed a small work shack off to the side. The woodshed, beside the house, was empty.

"Just about once a week, if I could, I'd make my way down the road to look in on them girls." Selma opened the unlocked door to the rundown farmhouse. "Ain't been here since that terrible day. Goodness. Been a year."

That cold feeling of isolation crept up my back. I asked her why she thought the Hinkle women's lives ended the way they did.

"Lord knows, what goes on in some folks' noggins. They

sure had a few bad turns. But then we all got that. Looka there, see, they had electricity and a space heater, but Carl said they stopped paying for the lights. They just did things their way." Her head bobbed as she spoke.

"They was gettin' pretty suspicious of everybody—didn't leave the house much. They weren't feelin' too fit in the last few years. I was worried on them. Health went up and down." Selma straightened items as she walked through the rooms, as if to make a difference. "Stubborn ole women. Pretty close, I'd say. Violet and Daisy took care of Rose. Her head was always in a cherry tree."

Selma shook her head, hard; loosening one of the tortoise shell hairpins in her tightly bound gray hair.

"Oh, my! It stinks awful in this house. Leave that door open."

I asked Selma why the house had not been cleaned and sold. Why was it sitting vacant?

"Waitin' for Lily to come back up here in spring and take care of business. Don't know why she hasn't been here fer over a year. I think she was just fed-up with the whole family. Funny stuff."

As I walked through the house, at first, I couldn't explain the discomfort. Was it fear? Was it the smell of death? What right did I have to invade this private crypt? I felt as if I were a guest going through my hosts' dresser drawers. I looked at the hall tree. Three straw bonnets hung waiting for the warmth of a summer day. Two hickory canes rested against a chair—maybe to help hardened hips? Three hand-knit sweaters hung under the hats. Selma said the Hinkles were skilled and talented craftswomen. I wondered if they showed their creations at county fairs. I asked Selma if she thought they were feminists. And what battles did they choose?

"Well, ain't that an odd question. Time was they was pretty busy gals. That Daisy was always writing letters to the big shots at the mines. They didn't like when she stirred the pot. She wrote letters right until she died."

I walked behind her silently, my thoughts jumping in all directions at each of her revelations. How long before that ill-fated day did their spirits die? Were they concerned how being dead spinsters in a news report would affect others?

The house was packed with all manner of clutter. The women seemed to have saved everything—tinfoil, string, bottles, magazines, newspapers, and stacks of books.

Selma pointed, and then sighed. "You know they found them 'round the stove back there in the kitchen. They was holdin' hands."

We both fell silent as we stared into the kitchen.

"Like I said, Lily, the youngest, is supposed to finally come and get rid of things in spring. She used to call them 'mule-headed hermits'. Don't seem right for kin to say such things. Don't seem right. She don't know all the happenings in this house. She were able to get away from the bad and hard times. Them sisters took their turn at misery. They protected their younger sister, Lily, from their father's roamin' hands."

*Roamin' hands?* I asked Selma what she meant.

Selma's face turned red as she spoke fiercely, "Well, Elsa Maas sez that Sam Hinkle figured he owned those women, and he could have his way with them. Stupid Lucille looked the other way. She should've protected those girls more. But, Elsa sez, when the two older girls were old enough, they protected Lily."

My heart pounded. My head supplied the details. I couldn't stand to hear this. I wanted to believe this secluded place was free of abuse and misery.

"Do you have kin, Miz Valente?" Selma asked, turning to look at me. "Are you doin' alright?"

I said I was fine, but a little overwhelmed. Then I told her I had a younger sister. I wanted to tell her about our three-year-old sister who died after she fell down a steep set of steps. My sister Carmela and I always felt pangs of guilt because we were supposed to have protected her.

*"Where were you two? How come you didn't watch her! You stupid tramps!"*

I remembered my mother screeching those hateful, hurtful words, but I couldn't remember Gioia's funeral. I couldn't remember much about her at all, even though I was eight when she died.

Selma nodded. "I get you. I had me three sisters and two brothers."

Selma Webster rattled on freely. She seemed to be aware of what I needed to hear in order to comprehend. I told her how much I appreciated her openness.

"I'm glad I can help. You know Lily felt real sad when Albert didn't push to get married. But twern't his fault. Ole Sam Hinkle didn't want his daughters gallivantin' around. That ole man gave Albert a hard time. That young'un, Lily, was so stuck on Albert an' Thomas Maas was stuck on her. But she didn't much care for him, you know, that way. A real merry-go-round. Ole lady Elsa Maas, she was as bad as Sam Hinkle. She didn't want her boys to marry. Hard to understand how some think."

Selma stopped to move a pile of rags that had fallen in her path.

"This has been one busy valley. Always somethin' happenin'. Then, not too long after that, Albert married the Bronson gal. Lily couldn't stand that. She got out fast. Left for the big city. Sam Hinkle wouldn't talk to her no more, after that. It all seemed to fracture the family."

Sam Hinkle sounded harsh and hard to handle, like my father, but I was glad I didn't have to deal with sexual abuse from my dad. This was the first I had heard about a marriage for Albert. Could this have been what he was reticent to share with me? I asked Selma if he was divorced.

"Oh! My, my, my, no!" she exclaimed. "Amy died all 'cause of what happened that black, evil day. No one likes to yarn about it. Albert suffered a long bit. Sat on his stoop lookin' out at the crick for days—just starin'—no talkin'—just starin'. Then, after Amy died, he gets in his car and leaves. Didn't come back for many a year—heard he went to some fancy school in New York City—got all educated and did some big work there. A coupla years ago, he came back, said he was done with that big city stuff."

Selma prattled on as she fluffed up the pillow on a chair, still trying to instill normalcy.

"Started fixin' the cottage by the crick. Says he was plannin' to live in the house ag'in. I sure don't see why. He's just about finished."

She became quiet. I wanted to ask what she meant by 'that black, evil day', but I knew she'd tell me in her own time.

"Now, there I go jawin' away—you came here to find out about the Hinkles, am I right?"

I nodded, and asked her if she minded my questions about the other villagers since they also had dealings with the Hinkles.

"Well, I guess. You're right there. It isn't as if our lives don't mix-up. And besides Albert was part of the community. But it's hard to talk about. Now, here's the little room Daisy liked to write in." Selma and I squeezed through the narrow doorway. "It's a jumble in here. Hardly room to walk. She liked to sit by that window to read and write. Spent many a year here. Mice just love this place. Who could blame them? They was never bothered."

A mess, indeed. Stacks of newspapers piled against each wall. On a small corner table, as if someone were keeping track, I glanced through an orderly stack of newspaper clippings of wedding announcements and obituary notices. My eyes darted from item to item, assessing reasons for them. People's lives connected like the web of a spider. I picked up the batch of death announcements and regarded the comments noted beside the name. Someone had underlined if the deceased had been married, along with the number of children. It was also recorded in the scrapbook, beside the clipped-out obituary, what illness the person had died from, and even if they were literate.

Written by one name: *Mother said she gave Mora and her brothers reading lessons in exchange for cabbage and potatoes.*

I considered what an interesting method this was to record particulars of one's existence.

I saw the corner of what looked like a diary. I picked up the inexpensive book with the generic brass hinge and thumbed through the volume. Written on the back in small numbers was *1986*. I didn't want to appear too eager at the discovery.

"Daisy kept those little books in her satchel everywhere she went. She kept a mess of them. I'll bet one for every year. She was a busy gal!"

I asked Selma what the Hinkles' social life had consisted of, or whether they'd always been reclusive.

"Not much for socializin'. I'm told that occasionally they'd go to dances when they was young. Wouldn't have nothin' to do with the Church. Sam Hinkle blamed preachers for not steppin' in to help the miners with negotiations. The Hinkle women always had somethin' homemade for the poor—gave them clothes and put up jars of fruits and vegetables. They all three were smart and like to read and write. Rose taught some of the workers for a while afore her ma died, but after that, the girls went to work in the garment factory, a few miles down the highway. They'd load into that rusty Pontiac in the shed and off they'd go to the job. At least it gave them a little retirement pension."

I noticed on one wall the faded family pictures of a time in the 1930's—when I was young. As far as I could see there were none of the Hinkle sisters. Each person in the photograph stood tall, colorless, and somber-faced.

Selma stopped to scan the photos with me. "Them ole pictures tell a lot of stories. Yes, ma'am. My mister told our boys, 'Get a job that pays benefits'. In those days miners had no health insurance, holidays off, or retirement plans, don'tcha know? He'd say, 'Get an education so you don't have to work with your backs and kill yourselves with coal dust. That ways you'll have enough money for a pine box in the end'. Yep, women were old afore their time, and men were dead afore theirs."

She turned from the pictures and looked into my eyes. Her finger waved in the air.

"Nobody knows the misery we went through. I hear the news today talk about women being raped and molested. *Huh,*" she scoffed. "They don't know nothin'. There were so many mothers, wives and daughters messed around with every day in these coal camps. These mine guards and company gunmen had them foreigners and us over a barrel. Tellin' us if we didn't give in, our men's jobs would be in trouble."

Sadness crept across Selma's face. I reached out and put my

arm about her shoulders. She was stiff, but still accepting. We talked for a while about crimes against the many females. I picked up a sense that I might be stirring up bad memories for her. Then I asked Selma if the sisters ever talked about their feelings or their lives. I wanted to know why they stopped functioning.

I saw similarities in their lives to my own life. I knew what it was like to be raised by an authoritarian father—one who would not allow my sister and me to date or to even talk to men. He was so strict and harsh that my mother, sister, and I feared his wrath.

Also, I had heard the all-too-vivid-stories my father told of his family's poverty in Italy and how difficult it was to find work in this country when he arrived from Europe. He worked from early morning until nightfall for a pittance and certainly no benefits. He had to learn English quickly to make his way. Prejudice was rampant and death came easily. It was a narrow window of belonging in the English speaking, white, 'man-of-means' world. We were, in many ways, like the Hinkles, the Fensters, the Schoens, the Websters, and the Maas family, struggling to stay above the prescribed six-feet of earth. Only the details were different.

"Well, you know like I said, Daisy liked to write more than Rose an' Violet," Selma said. "She wrote every spare minute. And she liked to keep scrapbooks. I think you saw a mess of them in that side room off the parlor. You know the little room we was just in.

"But 'twere Violet that were generally in control, just like her father. Violet made most of the decisions for them and the farm. Always screechin' out orders to the other two. She and Daisy would gather old sweaters, wash them and then pulled the yarn apart and used the wool to knit new goods for folks.

"Rose seemed to be pullin' away from everyone more and more in the last few years. I had the feelin' that somethin' happened to her. Always thinkin' in the past. Didn't talk as much as Violet and Daisy. They'd prattle away."

Selma found a chair and plopped. "Carl Fenster, you know he's the widower, paid them for the use of the land after they stopped plowin' it themselves, but Carl has been feelin' mighty bad since that awful day. He's of a mind that they became discouraged and gave up on livin' after he told them he wouldn't be farmin' their land, once the season was over. Grain prices went down, don't you know."

I asked her why there were so many elderly, unmarried women in the community. She watched me as I made my notes.

"Not hard to know. Being a spinster was not a thing that was looked on too favorably, but many girls rather have the single life than be like their mothers. In my mother's day a miner's wife worked pretty darn hard from dawn 'till dusk, havin' babies, housin' boarders, and all that work. Them women would make a little extra money cleanin' and feedin' single mine workers, superintendents or married men livin' without their families."

Selma's hands were lively as she relived memories.

"Them women had to wash all their oily laundry an' water was in short supply. Everyday she had to haul water down a ways. Them men had to bathe in a tub that she filled every night. She made meals and sent them to work each day with dinner buckets. It was like takin' care of an army. You hear plenty about how hard it was for the men in the mines, but how many know what was goin' on for these women in these coal dust covered shacks. It weren't tolerable. Listen to me goin' on."

She stood up. "You want to go in the kitchen?"

My knees were gelatinous as we went inside. The black and chrome wood stove dominated the square room. There was no other color. Limp dirty lace curtains showed slight signs of a healthier time. I looked at a washed out 1981 calendar with cherubs playing in clouds. The counters near the sink displayed decayed food where mice and humans nourished themselves.

Selma and I stood motionless. I held onto the back of a chair. It was a smell of staleness. A death smell. I felt sick.

I could almost hear the Hinkle sisters' final thoughts as they surrounded the iron heart of the kitchen. They clustered together as they sat on the floor, purposely placing their legs under the warmth of the stove. Violet and Daisy each clasped Rose's hands. Rose's body had fallen and had lain across their laps. How long did they wait for the last embers? I stood entranced as tears rose to my eyes.

Why? I wanted to know. *What were your thoughts that day—why did you give up—what made the difference in your lives—and what guilts and agonies did you take with you when you died?*

The ancient kitchen had open shelves of dust encased unmatched chipped, dishware, miscellaneous Mason jars of peaches, string beans, and corn gone bad, pickles and sauerkraut. A small pile of flour sat on a wooden board where someone had attempted to make bread. Mice droppings were everywhere.

Selma left the kitchen. I followed. I asked her if I could look at the scrapbooks.

"Well, now, I guess 'twould be all right. But I wouldn't want you to take any papers or anything. Hope you don't mind me sayin'. They was mighty strange, wouldn't you say, Miz Valente?"

I nodded and offered that most of us are peculiar with our needs and dreams.

"Well, that's a truth. Now, Miz Valente, I have to pick up my grandbabies from the school bus stop. My daughter's a maid for the motel in Pine Grove Haven, so I try to help her as much as possible. Awful hard for her since her man was kilt last year. Drove a semi. Fell asleep at the wheel. Mighty thankful he didn't hit anyone."

I struggled for words to offer condolences.

"Thank you, 'twere bad. Children pine terribly." Grief lines circled her eyes. "Lot of us widows here. Awful lots. It's a dyin' town. Will you be all right alone here for a spell?" Selma asked. "Are you sure you're warm enough? I suppose you can leave in that nice car of yours when you're tired. Just pull the door closed. I brought you a thermos of coffee and a coupla cookies in this wax paper."

I thanked her and told her I would be fine. Her aged car drove away on the frozen mud road. I gazed out of the clouded window, my warm breath steaming the icy cold pane. Unexpectedly, I felt like a frightened child, remembering when my parents left me alone to attend to their errands. Alone. Could I have managed my life as well as Selma and the Hinkle women?

I went back into the kitchen and stared at the stove again, imagining the sisters holding hands for their final moments, hugging the warmth that was familiar to them as babies and little girls. Suddenly, I was worried that I would someday end up sad and alone. Would my archaeologist understand me and my trappings?

To leave this world singly and unscheduled is bad enough, but what made these women choose to depart this existence together? How does one get up one morning and say, "We are through—today we die." Did they know each other's secrets? Did they know what they wanted their lives to be? Was there a timid one who went along not to make waves? How many of us let others run our lives—too fearful to risk our own steps?

I walked back to the alcove next to the living room. Set against the windowsill, was another rough-hewn table four feet square that held a stack of writings, papers and journals. Light beamed through the frost-edged windows onto the string-bound pages.

I sat on a wooden chair and swept the dust from the manuscripts, but I was hesitant to open them. I gazed out at the cold, stark scene of brittle trees. Except for the wail of a bitter wind that had begun to blow from the upper hill down into the ravine, everything seemed lifeless. Fifty feet away, a fox seemed to focus on its prey, scampered close to the ground. I thought of how the women could have watched this same fox, or its family, as it caught a rabbit, watched the unwary meal as it struggled and fought for its survival.

I rubbed my thighs to generate heat, then, hesitantly, I untied the pages and began to read. I guessed it was Daisy, who had written these stories and poems. The accounts were mainly of the coalminers' countless efforts—written with simplicity and vision, belief, and justice. There were stories where the spirit still longed for the finer things in life, such as poetry, art, and song. I read until the light dimmed. She had written what seemed a semi-fictional history of her community. I couldn't tell where the fine line between truth and storytelling lay. Daisy had chronicled the heartbreaks and tragedies and how they affected the families.

I was amazed at my feelings. I didn't need to travel out of my country to see and understand poverty. I felt I was in a time warp that drew me back to a cut in the earth's crust surrounded by bustling cities of progress. Here we were in the twentieth century and the dormant rusted mineshafts and equipment reminded me of the saga of sweat and exertion. It was as real today as it had been a thousand years ago. Fears and mores ground out harsh paths for the tenants of Pine Grove Haven.

The diary and scrapbooks marked the sisters' existence. I wondered where the other diaries were. Selma didn't say. Possibly hidden. I would need to come back and look through the house. I skimmed through the yellowed pages, not sure of what I expected to see, or what I wanted to see. Would I find one story about the Hinkle women that would give me a crisp picture of their lives?

I sat on the hard-spindled chair, suddenly realizing I was dreadfully cold. I opened the thermos and poured a welcome cup of Selma's hot coffee.

The signature on the stories, Daisy Maude Hinkle, was in a barely legible scrawl. As yet the narratives told me nothing about their family, but some plots seemed familiar. I quickly sifted through the pages of one story written and dated many years before, called *Mourning*. It appeared to be about a family who lost their only two children and how difficult it was for their mother to continue without them. It intrigued me. I would need to come back and read more.

I looked at my watch and realized I had been glued to my seat for close to three hours reading these pieces of paper. I left the writings for a while and walked about the house just to get a sense of their personal effects—what they had saved and felt was valuable, the type of books they read. The women were obviously enthusiastic readers. I wondered how they got their education.

I nearly fell to my knees when I heard the three raps on the entry door and then it opened.

"You in there, Miz Valente?"

It was Carl Fenster.

"You're gonna catch your death. Once that sunlight goes, she drops down right fast!" He looked at me with concern. "Whatcha' doin' in here? Whatcha think you be findin'? Some mystery?"

I told him I was about ready to leave for the day and shared with him my thoughts about Daisy's writings.

"Now, they was simple folks, don'tcha know? Nothing fancy, but proud. Daisy, she were a good one to make up things in her noggin'. I don't know how she'd come up with all the stuff. Got herself in trouble a few times for speakin' out of turn."

This intrigued me. I asked Carl what he meant by speaking out of turn.

"She were a rabble-rouser at one time. Stuck her nose in men's business. She were mad about the way they run things down at the mine. Got on picket lines. Now, don't get me wrong, there was certainly enough to complain about, but it sure didn't seem right for a girl to churn the waters. Made us men look bad. Like we couldn't do our own biddin'. Some of these modern wimmin' think they're wearin' the pants."

I stayed quiet, listening to his heated words. I asked him if any of the men stood up for themselves.

"Well, hell! We barely had time to eat! Tweren't nobody!"

I suggested maybe Daisy's speaking out was really a good thing, that she understood that the men had enough to do to keep going and could use help. He apologized for losing his temper. I could see his regret was true.

"My Dora didn't take guff from anybody. She were a fighter too, just like them Hinkle girls. Women have to be strong here. They're the ones has to do most work above ground."

I told him about the story I read, the one called *Mourning.*

"Well, now, like I said, she had a hellava 'magination. Those girls were smart. Yesireee, smart."

He seemed to dance around many of my questions.

I wanted to know if the others in the community had liked them. Was there any reason that he could think of that may have isolated the family?

"Well, I can't rightly say. They was helpful when folks needed. But they missed a lot of life because of their pa's strictness and heavy hand. He kept an eye on them. Scuffed them around a bit if they didn't do as he wanted. Even after Sam died they acted like he was still in charge. But we all had a rough road to cut through."

Carl was avoiding my interest in the story of the two children. He took off one glove and poked a finger inside his ear. I wanted to know if this was an account that he was familiar with.

"Well, now, we've all had our bad news. Some things are best left alone."

I stood up and stretched. The farmhouse creaked with the wind as if stretching along with me. I asked Carl Fenster what Mrs. Hinkle was like.

"Lucille? Well, she was an alright lady. Her ma and pa didn't like Sam Hinkle. Weren't too happy when she married him. I remember it said how she'd go over to their place, bring them vittles, clean their house, wash their clothes and work her fingers 'til they was raw for her folks and they wouldn't talk to her. Wouldn't even talk to her daughters. Shame how families think. They lived to a ripe old age."

I couldn't help but think how we humans were interesting

pieces of this earth, always looking into other people's lives and business, measuring and competing for the final tally. Conquering each other to claim land, property, and positions, and always, always the need to be right.

Masking the real need.

The need to love and be loved.

I told him a little about my own background of alienation from my father and mother. It was a life of rejection and bitterness, because I wouldn't jump through their many hoops. We all were similar, in one way or another, I said to Carl.

He nodded his head in agreement. His stern eyes had softened.

I buttoned my jacket and put on my gloves. Carl held the door for me.

"Say, Miz Valente, I hear you're havin' dinner with Pastor Miller and his wife Nell, tonight. She's a good girl."

## *Excerpts from the Diaries of Miss Daisy Maude Hinkle*

### 1922—July

There is no doubt that Rose likes to teach. She seems to enjoy giving reading and writing lessons to the coal miners and their families. I know if she could have had a better education she would have been a fine teacher.

But she hasn't been acting well for sometime. I think something has happened to her. I've asked her, but she won't answer. She's one to keep thoughts to herself. I know she still pines for our brother, Zachary.

Violet is already twenty-seven and it doesn't look like she'll marry. Ma doesn't talk to her much. There seems to be a strain between them. Sometimes I think Ma is jealous because Pa likes to talk politics with us. Violet used to say, when we were young, that she wanted to be a doctor. Ma laughed and said,

"No chance of that! You might as well ask to be Queen!" Everyone seems stuck with their unfulfilled dreams in this valley.

•

**1922—August**

It has been a mean summer. Ma is mad at Rose and won't have anything to do with her. She calls her names. It just isn't fair. Why are our lives so complicated?

•

**1923—February**

Lily was born yesterday. She's so sweet and tiny—almost like a doll. Elsa delivered her.

•

**1925—May**

Ma goes to Grandma's and Grandpa's house just about every day to help with chores. They won't talk to Ma much and they never ask about us—they don't care for us. They are still mad that Ma married our pa. They hold bitterness a long time.

•

**1926—June**

I never see anybody paint their houses. No one can afford paint—but it would be so nice to see things prettied up. There is so little beauty here. Sometimes when I look at books I see the beautiful houses, cottages, and green lush gardens of England and I wish I were born elsewhere.

I wonder if everyone on earth has as much sadness as we have.

# *Chapter 4*
# *Decrees*

"Nell, give that lady another piece of upside-down cake. I don't think they know how to feed 'em out there in Seattle." Preacher Miller gave a thunderous snort. He leaned back in the oak chair and looked at his wife of forty years. "Nell can whip up a meal with just shavins'. People think you can't be happy unless you have children, but we've proved them wrong. Isn't that right, Nell?"

Mrs. Miller, deathly thin, the bones of her chest standing out, quietly moved about, but didn't answer her rotund, scaly-skinned husband.

"She lost three. Two others were stillborn," he stated matter-of-factly, as though talking about his livestock.

I was shocked at the exposure of his wife's privacy. I looked at Mrs. Miller and acknowledged how difficult that must have been. I told her of my one loss of a baby boy, and that I thought that was bad enough. Tears filled her eyes—she was careful not to let them flow. I wondered if she was as happy as Pastor Miller maintained they were.

"Graveyard's filled with scores of babes that never got to walk," he offered readily.

We talked for a bit. I felt a nudge of discomfort in asking questions. Even so, I took my chance to inquire if he knew anything about Daisy's writings and her diaries.

"What? I knew she wrote news articles, but I didn't know anythin' about her writin' in diaries. I can't imagine what she had to write about," he replied. "I know she liked to stir-the-pot with her letters regardin' problems with the mines. I'll say this, Miz Valente, we've had our share of misfortunes and scandals, I suppose. But it's no *Peyton Place* if you're lookin' for juicy fruit for a romance novel."

"Now, Cyrus, let Miz Valente ask her questions," Mrs. Miller spoke up, as she swept the cake crumbs from the tablecloth. Her dress hung on her frame as if on a wire hanger.

I realized I had struck a tender topic. Pastor Miller eased his taut, white clerical collar. His face was engorged like a puffer fish.

"Now, woman, you mind yerself. Get these dishes off this table!" he ordered, his bald head turning redder.

The tenseness and mood change was discomforting and reminiscent of my own past. My mother would not have dared to contradict my father. I changed the subject and talked in generalities about the mines and the people. I knew I would have to go elsewhere to find out more.

Around seven o'clock, soon after dinner, the phone rang. Pastor Miller answered.

"Well, I must go. Ole Mrs. Hatcher is close to leavin' us,"

he announced, after he'd hung up the phone. "Miz Valente, I'm sure you'll be needin' to get back to your motel room soon. Mind these icy back roads, one wrong turn and you'll land in a gully. You could be there for days and no one would find you."

His wife interrupted his litany and said, "Stay a while longer, Miz Valente. I'll make us some tea."

As he buttoned his heavy down parka, Pastor Miller remarked sternly, "Now, Nell, you must be tired. Don't forget we have a big day tomorrow with the church bazaar. We have a lot of money to raise. You're invited to come, Miz Valente, if you'd like. A good way to meet new folk."

I thanked him for the invitation.

"We'll be fine, Cyrus. Send prayers to the Hatchers." Nell closed the door and relaxed.

I saw her bolster courage to continue our talk.

"I'll just pour us more hot water from the kettle and then we can sit in the parlor."

Nell went about her tasks with precise movements. Her sparse salt and pepper hair was cropped short, parted in the middle, and caught behind her ears. Round wire rimmed glasses resting on her straight nose, framed her unblinking eyes. Her face lacked smile lines.

"Sit in that, it's more comfortable," she said pointing to a worn, overstuffed, armchair from the thirties. She pulled her rocker closer, set her lean body down, and reached into a basket for her crocheting. "I make gifts to sell at the bazaar. I just need to finish these potholders for tomorrow's sale. Do you mind, Miz Valente?"

I shared that my maternal grandmother and aunt were quite talented with their handmade needlework and said I occasionally found pleasure in it as well.

"Are you gettin' to understand the Hinkle girls, yet?" By now, Nell was quite willing to have conversation. "Maybe not much to know, I 'spect. I knew about them writin'. 'Twere mostly Daisy, don'tcha know. We ladies always know the goin's on in these small communities. How else to ease pain? Men don't bother with women's talk. They think we don't ponder beyond the kitchen, but word gets about in these close hills."

Nell put her handwork down to sip some of the strong black tea. She didn't seem intimidated since her husband left. I told her I believed women were the conduits of the planet and that men could learn a great deal from our capabilities and logic.

"Well, now, don't that square just right. Men are strong when they're haulin' and turnin' the world upside down, but when they get older they're more easily broken. They couldn't hold together if they was losin' babies. Nosireee."

I looked at her vacant eyes. She momentarily withdrew. Each time the people of this valley revealed a piece of themselves I saw the connection to my own small world. I often wondered if anyone suspected what brutality was going on in my family. My parents didn't allow their dirty secrets to go out the door. We could never allow our make-believe to be pierced. How shattering would it have been to let our friends know of our sickly love? Our fake and destructive life? Our lack of trust for each other?

"Miz Valente," Nell started, "I think I know about the story you mentioned before. It's about the two Schoen tots, ain't it?"

I replied that I didn't know. I asked myself, the Schoen children? Could they be Martha and John's? I told her about Daisy's story called *Mourning,* but the name used wasn't Schoen. I asked Nell to tell me the story she was referring to.

"Well, now, this happened to the Schoens a good many year ago. But these young'uns were not Martha and John's. They was Albert's."

I sat unable to answer immediately. Then I remembered my conversation with Selma Webster about what she called 'that black evil day'. I gulped my tea and told Nell that I had wondered about Albert.

"Yes, he married that young Amy Bronson girl. This Amy was a looker, sometimes a little wild. Couldn't seem to settle down at first, but after she had her children she straightened out. Turned out a good mother. Albert fixed that cottage by the crick. They was doing good. When he heard she was gonna have twins, he was the happiest man around! Would you like me to heat your tea up a bit? It'll be a while until Cyrus comes home. Could be there all night."

I told her more tea would be fine. I pulled my cardigan close around me. I could feel the cold air seeping in under the door and around the windows, even though it was blocked with wads of cloth. It was as if the news of the evening brought the chill with it. Nell returned with two fresh cups of tea.

"Can't seem to stop this cold from reachin' us. Now, where was I? Oh, yes. Well, Amy had the dear babes, a girl, Glenna Sue, and boy, Albert Jr. For extra money, Albert would teach at a private school in Harrisburg. He were a smart man. A good man, but stubborn," she hesitated, "always in charge. Kept his thoughts in a straight line. Never wandered. It shouldn't of happened to him."

I felt my brain begin to shut down. I wasn't sure if I could handle hearing this story.

"Anyway, the way I knowed it, the five-year-old twins were playin' in the garden that spring day. We just had us a terrible rain. It flooded part of the valley. Amy was in the house. Now, nobody knows who it was in there with her. Some say she was playin' tiddily winks, but waggin' tongues aren't satisfied unless they suckin' bitter gumdrops. Whoever the man was, as some claim there was, he high-tailed it out the front when Amy tried to go outside. Some say it was ole Calvin Mooney, Clive Mooney's father. He used to help us all with repairs. Sometimes he'd take his son, Clive, with him to help out on jobs. Amy was kind to their family, always cookin' somethin' for them to take home. Calvin lost his wife from consumption."

I gasped. My shoulders tightened as I pressed my hands between my knees.

"Amy heard her young son yellin' for help, and she ran out the back door to the yard. She saw her boy standin' on a rock at the crick's edge tryin' to reach for somethin', but afore she could get to him, he slipped into the fast runnin' water. He'd been reachin' for his sister."

We sat silent. My heart thumped. I was involved with these people. I wasn't just reading an article in the newspaper. I would never read anything again about this region of the country without feeling the depth of their lives. Nell looked at me and realized how affected I was.

"Are you sure you're up to hearin' this yarn?"

I nodded.

"Well, you know, Miz Valente, no one talks about this anymore. Haven't for a far time."

I asked her why she trusted telling me this dreadful story.

"Well, I think folks should know the truth, don't you? I think I'm a pretty good judge of character and if you're the sort that'll do evil to someone, then you'll get your comeuppance in the end. Isn't that right?"

I agreed and thought of the amazing innate wisdom that pervaded these hills.

Nell continued with the particulars surrounding Amy and Albert, "Like I said, whoever it was in that house with Amy must have slipped away quick-like. Amy jumped into the crick to save those young'uns, but the water was too swift and she couldn't catch them. Afore you knew it, the babies was taken downstream."

Her head shook from side to side.

"*Mmmm,*" she moaned. "We could hear her screamin' that day, from farm to farm. Sometimes God forgets us small people."

Nell stopped to remove her glasses and dabbed at the corners of her eyes.

"Our volunteer rescue crew came, but it weren't no use. Thomas Maas found the dead babes under Stoneman Bridge, tucked together near a boulder." She paused, then said, "Folks said they was holdin' hands."

I couldn't stop the flow of tears. I looked at Nell. Her eyes were filled again with the pain yet still she was unable to cry.

"Amy didn't leave the house much, ag'in. The sorrow and shame was just awful. That house shuddered with agony. They say she got herself so down in the dumps, wouldn't eat and drank herself to death." Nell gave her head another shake.

"Albert heard the rumors of man seen runnin' out of the house, but didn't know who it was for sure. He was bitter at Amy because she wouldn't sat who was there, or what was going on. She told him only that there was a visitor, but that nothing was out of order. He didn't believe her. He pleaded with her to tell him who it was. She refused. Then he started listenin' to the town's waggin' tongues. After Amy died, Albert sat, every minute he could by the crick—just starin'."

I put my hand to my mouth to muffle the guttural sound that was coming from the deepest part of me.

**Venera Di Bella Barles**

# *Excerpts from the Diaries of Miss Daisy Maude Hinkle*

## 1928—May

I met a young woman today, a reporter working for the newspaper in Philadelphia. She was writing an article about the strikes. We chatted about how she started writing. I told her some of my ideas and desire to write stories. She said that I should put them down and take the idea of writing seriously. She pointed out that living in a situation like this coal-mining community there must be all kinds of accounts that I could write about. Funny I never thought that I could maybe do something like this. I always thought I was silly to think that I had anything to say or even put down my thoughts. She said I should try to send them in to the Philadelphia paper to see if they could be published. I'm so excited. Tomorrow I will start.

**1939—October**

Pa is angry with Lily. He says she acts too independent for a girl. He found out she wants to go to a barn dance with Albert. Thomas likes Lily too, but Mrs. Maas doesn't want her boys dallying with girls. If Lily doesn't go away she'll end up like Rose, Violet, and me. I don't like it when Pa gets upset.

When Rose is feeling herself, she makes a little spare change helping those men and boys with their studies.

Sure good that we get those old books at Henley's Thrift store. We picked up some fine ones today.

•

**1939—November**

I've had quite a few commentaries and stories accepted and published in the past ten years. I only wish I could get my anthologies in print. There is hardly a chance there. I have been sending my pieces of writings to the Pittsburgh Post-Gazette. It looks like they may take my last commentary. I've been using only my initials, D. M. Hinkle. I think that helps—this is still a man's world. I know I shouldn't feel so excited, but I can't resist the reaction. Ma says I'm always wasting my time.

# Chapter 5
# The Conduits

During my sleepless night, I played the scenarios of the last couple of days over and over in my head. This was nuts, I thought. Tragedies and difficult lives were everywhere. What made this so different? Was it the remoteness of this sort of community? How interesting that we seem to fall back to our cave-dwelling ancestors and cling closer together to insure a modicum of safety from strangers and intruders. Misfortunes stand out more when people know each other.

The next morning, the air was biting. I had forgotten the sensation of intensely cold winters. The car took forever to warm up. Through the fogged windshield, I saw the white steeple of Pine Grove Haven church.

As I parked my car, I noticed through my window the bobbing heads of close conversations. I walked indoors and made my rounds to the variety of tables showing the church women's diverse talents—cakes, pies, jars of jam, vegetables, knitted slippers, caps, and aprons.

"Miz Valente, let me put those doll clothes in a sack for you," offered Martha Schoen. "Do your granddaughters enjoy playin' with dolls?"

I nodded and told her they loved their dolls.

"Well, now, that's nice. Mary Lou Hendricks makes them. Has won ribbons for her fine handwork. She always donates to the church bazaar."

She paused momentarily to look at me.

"I understand you had dinner last night with Nell and Reverend Miller. Learned a lot, I suppose. Pastor had to look in on Miz. Hatcher, I hear."

Everyone knew everything immediately, a much more efficient system than my postal service at home. I confirmed her assumptions. As I paid and thanked Martha for the petite dresses, I looked about and could see almost everyone from the township was out for the event. The bitter cold had forced the parishioners into the church's community room.

I had already been there a week and knew I might have to extend my stay. The people of the valley—sometimes directly or indirectly, made inquiries into what I might write in my book. I assured them they would all remain anonymous if I was to use any of the facts I had garnered. In spite of trepidations, I sensed their trust and felt an awareness of belonging. They owed me neither of these. There were also suspicious reactions from some, because a stranger, like me, was interested in their stories.

I turned back to Martha and saw her brother-in-law, Albert, across the room. His eyes seemed to penetrate me. I didn't know how long he had been standing there. I felt that pang of uneasiness again, a feeling of having poked my nose into crypt secrets. I immediately acknowledged him. He smiled and tipped his small-brimmed, Swiss-style fedora. His response calmed me. I debated about telling him what I had heard about his family. I couldn't make believe I didn't know—how complicated it all was! I now was enmeshed in their lives, worrying about feelings, caring what impression I was making.

Albert came towards me and chortled lightheartedly, "Ms. Valente, are you enjoying our gala affair? You don't want to miss these big to-dos. They are the highlight of our winter. Helps the cabin-fever and breaks the repetitiveness of our lives."

I smiled and acknowledged him. He towered over me as he spoke in his warm reassuring way. I wondered why he would return to this sorrowful zone of memories. He seemed out of place in this area.

"Are you finding it difficult to put together notes regarding the Hinkles?" the polished Albert asked. "In their younger years, it's said, they were a lively family. I certainly know they had sorrows like the rest of us."

I told him there was much to learn about the women. How they lived and interacted in Pine Grove Haven. I mentioned looking through their house and coming across the intriguing scrapbooks and writings.

"Oh? That does sound interesting. I wasn't aware of that. After their mother died, they became quite reclusive. God only knows why. People do think in mysterious ways, don't they?"

I nodded.

"They're serving hot cider down at the other end. Care to have a cup?"

I quickly agreed. Maybe, I thought, I could inform him of

my visit with Nell. He took my arm and led me to an area with tables and chairs. I sensed the watchful eyes and twisting heads as Albert escorted me with slow deliberate steps. He had certain energy, an energy of quiet strength.

"Ms. Valente, I know you'll be leaving in a few days," he said as he removed his hat and placed it on a vacant seat, "but I guarantee that it will not matter whose home you visit nor to whom you speak, they will all have lived hard and, for many, desperate lives. Our valley is, for the most part, a ghostly place. Misery is imbedded in these refuse piles we call homes."

He poured the hot cider, handed me the drink, and then sat across from me. His gaze steadily held mine. What was that feeling? I felt a sudden disquiet, then a flush of warmth. I could feel my cheeks brightening.

"Are you doing all right, Ms. Valente? Is there anything I can get you?"

I assured him I was fine, just adjusting to a momentary chill but knowing inwardly that this man had touched a sensual cell in my body. I smiled with my trivial daydream. I was too old for this nonsense. I was through with relationships. I didn't need to start up anything new at this stage of life. Since my husband's death ten years ago, I'd had several male companions, but the only serious one, four years ago, ended amicably.

"Tell me about yourself," he asked. "What about this story made you interested enough to come this distance?"

As nearly as I could put into words, for I knew I didn't fully understand why myself, I told him what it was that intrigued me about the deaths of the three women. I couldn't imagine what it was that allowed them to consider death as an option to solving difficulties. I let him know that I planned to revisit the Hinkle farmhouse, possibly tomorrow. Then I asked him if he would be willing to talk about his association with the family.

"Well, yes. Except for the time I lived in New York City, I knew them most of my life. But, I only really knew Lily, since she was more my age and we went to the same school. Her sisters were much older."

He looked around as if to check who was observing us. "We have quite a gossip conduit in this community. Does it make you uncomfortable sitting here with me?"

I knew he was aware of what I was thinking. His grin spoke volumes. He was having a fun shot at flirting. I revealed that there was a *slight* discomfort but that we were just sitting and talking as I have conversed with many in the area. He continued telling me about his connection with Lily and her family.

"Her father was terribly strict and wouldn't let her go out with boys. I tried to approach him, but he was determined to keep a tight leash on the girls. Yet, with it all, Lily got through her education. Lily seemed embarrassed about her family. She didn't like talking about them."

He was careful—careful not to get too detailed. I sensed a sudden disquiet in his voice. I wanted to tell him of my conversation with Nell Miller about his children and wife, but I knew I would have to wait for a better opportunity. I asked instead about his relationship with Lily Hinkle.

"That's hard to say. It was a very long time ago and much has happened since those innocent days. I cared for her a great deal. I know I was her first love."

He looked at me, checking to see how I received this news. I momentarily recalled my first love and how difficult it had been for me. I was sixteen, and he was fifteen-years older. I wasn't allowed to date or have boyfriends and my whole dating life was in secret. When the man found out that I was underage, he said we shouldn't see each other any longer. I wept for months.

Albert leaned back in his chair. "Lily and I would meet secretly when we were able, but I knew that I couldn't keep up the covert play without encountering trouble. Even Thomas Maas tried to take her to barn dances, but her father, Sam, shooed him away. Sam was extremely protective of his daughters—maybe a little too shielding. Lucille, their mother, didn't intervene to help them. I felt bad for Lily. Sometimes she had some pretty mean bruises on her—Ms. Valente, you have tears in your eyes, is something wrong?"

I told him I was all right and that I understood. I explained that I, too, had a similar first love, and that my father also was dreadfully heavy-handed. He was careful to not let me have any male friends. I hated the secrecy of my life.

How strange this all felt. What was I doing? Telling confidences I had carefully shrouded. This quiet place harbored the deepest emotions. These past few days had raised a world of feelings for everyone. The three dead women had elicited issues in me I thought long dead. I revealed more to these citizens than I had even to close friends.

"I once heard that life, with its stunning moments, has a way of interrupting an otherwise meaningless existence. We have all had our stunning moments, haven't we?" he said in a tranquil voice.

I could not hold back any longer. I had to tell him how dreadfully sorry I was. I took a deep breath and declared to him that I had heard the awful truth of the loss of his wife and children.

His vibrant figure slumped.

"Ah, yes, I wondered when you would hear of that unbearable heartbreak. There are a great many ill-advised talking heads that can cause disgusting pain." He paused, and then sighed. "Did you know that the world *can* end in a day?"

He dropped his eyes then raised them to a space above my head. His face tightened. I could see the trembling movement of his jaw. He was obviously struggling to lighten the matter. He looked off as if he couldn't bear to meet my eyes.

"How I loved them."

# *Excerpts from the Diaries of Miss Daisy Maude Hinkle*

**1941—December**

The Japanese have bombed an American base in Hawaii.

Now Hitler and Mussolini have declared war on the U.S. I cannot believe we are going to war again!

Some of the miners' boys will be going to service. Young Albert Schoen and Thomas Maas will be leaving soon. There will be many young men and women going to serve.

•

**1942—May**

Elsa Maas came to visit Ma today. She said she needed Violet to help keep an eye on a miner's wife who was pretty ill after delivery. Elsa has helped many women with their babies. Our babies, too. She doesn't take any backtalk from anybody. Awfully strong, one has to be strong here. She always says, "Ain't nobody gonna get out of here alive – you might as well do it right!"

Medicine is scarce here. The company store is strict with supplies. Mrs. Erwin's twins are sick with whooping cough. She's mighty scared that they will die like her other child. A lot of the children seemed to be coming down with this. Elsa Maas is certainly a blessed angel. She has helped so many. I can tell she misses Thomas. It must be lonely for her without him.

It's a good thing Pa can sell those vegetables. It helps with extras.

•

**1943—June 20th**

Pa is dead. Pa is dead.

They pulled Pa and some other workers out of the hole. They say that he survived the blast, but died of suffocation from gas. It's been a couple of weeks and some men are still down there behind the cave-in. They don't think any of them are alive.

I read in the newspaper that the families of miners never forget a mine experience. After a deafening explosion—the mine fills with a thunderbolt of light. Then a booming wall of flame destroys everyone and everything in its course. It then becomes a calamitous firestorm.

We buried Pa yesterday. Ma said we all have to take care of things now that he's gone. No one talks about Pa. Rose is very quiet. Violet just makes believe everything is normal.

Lily left again today to get back to her job. If she only knew everything that has happened in our lives. It's just as well. Why should everyone be miserable?

I don't know how I feel. At least he can't hit or bother us any longer. I know I'm scared. If there is a God, he certainly has singled us out to be tested. Sometimes I think God is just a big story to scare us all.

Carl Fenster said he could plow our fields, and then we'll be able to still sell the vegetables at market. Said he could have his little boys' help. Dora Fenster and other ladies have been sending over food for us.

I heard Ma crying last night.

# Chapter 6
# Mourning: The Heart of the Matter

The house was even colder than before, but it wasn't the temperature that gave me gooseflesh; it was the isolation of it all. Nothing could warm the penetrating loneliness. Down in this narrow valley, the Hinkles hid from their own community. Sam Hinkle bought the remote piece of property, located away from other tenants of the patch, built the two-story house, and added to it as the family grew. The daily walk to the mineshaft must have been long and difficult.

I pulled the flashlight from my purse, I wanted to see the family's sleeping quarters, so I crept slowly up the narrow wooden staircase, realizing as I climbed how often the Hinkles ritualistically did the same. Smudges on the ancient flowered wallpaper illustrated balance patterns. The wide sawn-wood floors creaked as I walked around the three small rooms. The only bed that appeared to have been used was a full-size metal frame one with springs and a sagging mattress.

The window, under the gable, faced the woods and a fork of Black Creek—which I found out from the map I kept in my purse. It looked like a rustic painting with its surrounding pinewood frame. It had never been painted, and the yellowed lace curtain had been nailed into place. I shuddered when I opened a small armoire with only two pieces of dated clothing outfits; a black suit for a man and a black dress for a woman. Two pairs of black shoes were at the bottom. Two black hats were on the shelf.

Spider webs waited for their seasonal tenants.

In my snooping and searching, behind the bed stand covered with candles and melted wax, I found a short door in the wall that led to a storage closet. I flashed the small searchlight about. In the midst of the stacks of books there was a box of Daisy's other diaries. On the outside of the back covers, they were labeled by years. I gasped when reality set in. A whole life lay within these miniature journals. I thumbed through several of them and then took out three or four to take downstairs to study. I was more curious about the years before their deaths and the years surrounding the deaths of the Schoen twins.

My eyes centered on the drooping bed and wondered if Violet, Daisy, and Rose slept together for warmth or security, and who got the middle?

Oh, how I hated sleeping between my father and mother as a small girl. The suffocating, claustrophobic feeling still choked my breathing when I got in tight places.

I found my chest feeling tighter just thinking about it.

My mind filled with mixed thoughts. Every time I read or heard something about the people in this town, I found myself flashing back to times of my youth.

After I sat a moment to clear my head, I wandered back through the rooms. They were simple—no knick-knacks or frivolous touches. All the niceties they had made with their hands had been given to others, or else just put away. Did anyone ever try to break the mold? I knew what an oppressor's attitude was like in our home. My father's need for control dominated our thinking. I realize that's what wiped out my mother's desire for parenting and homemaking.

For so long, in those young years, I was angry at her for not saving us, not realizing she was part of the malignancy. It took my unfortunate breakdown, after marriage and childbirth and years of therapy to see the different parts we were all playing to keep the cancer alive. When my eyes finally opened, I saw the disease in most families.

How amazed I was that my thoughts kept jumping to my own past.

I returned downstairs to the alcove to look through more of the scrapbooks. Again, I saw accounts of lives in photos and articles illustrating the hardships of the miners and their families. There were pages of obituaries of the mine-related deaths, through accident or disease. Babies and mothers who died in childbirth for lack of medical care. I perceived a longing in the carefully documented gathering of marriage announcements and photographs. At first I had difficulty determining who was doing the collecting. As I leafed through the papers, I began to recognize that most, if not all, were Daisy's writings.

Unexpectedly, I came across an article dated April 30, 1952. The day of my birthday.

**FIVE-YEAR-OLD TWINS DROWN IN SPRING-SWOLLEN BLACK CREEK.**

My throat tightened as I read the wretched report. Why is it, when we read the printed word, even if there are distortions, it seems much more bona fide? As I scanned the story, I was horrified.

A female witness was interviewed:

> "I was driving my momma in the old Chrysler to her quilting guild meeting that day, and we was going right by Schoens' cottage. I looked and saw a man hightail it out the front door, couldn't tell who he was. He were young, I think, anyways he left the door wide open. I could hardly see the car he was running to. It was hiding under the trees on the side of the house. Who knows? Some say she was a fast girl. Maybe that was her sweet patootie."

I read on. The way the account was written sparked anger in me. I hated finger pointing and the damage it brought. It placed tremendous guilt upon Amy, the children's mother. What evidence was there that she had betrayed her husband and was so negligent and preoccupied that she allowed her twins to die?

I wanted to sort out the truth of everything I learned, but it was as if I were slugging away in a hot-glue pot. I came for one story regarding the Hinkle women, but now my thinking had become fragmented. No one gets through this life without being touched by someone else—not even hermits.

Since I hadn't finished reading Daisy Maude Hinkle's short story, *Mourning,* I took a few minutes to do so. The basic description was quite similar to the Schoen catastrophe, but it did not place guilt on the character resembling Amy. When I finished the chronicle, I was taken aback at the particulars surrounding the so-called male visitor. Daisy was doing her best to disguise the man's identity. All was not as it seemed.

Dazed, I got up and walked about the room. The stench of death and mustiness in the closed house lessened. I leaned my forehead against an old, bubbled windowpane and gazed at the rust-cankered plow, forever frozen in the field. All around me were the trappings of these people and the evidence of an abandoned household—scarred and dented pots and pans, corroded sewing needles, overgrown gardens, worn utensils, encrusted machinery—all that the Hinkle women held dear and endeavored to preserve. All ended in the wink of that fatal day's decision.

In reading, I was convinced that Daisy knew what actually had happened on the day of the terrible creek accident. She wove the particulars into her story. There were those questions again. Who had she learned the details from? Or, maybe, she just had an active imagination.

I needed air. I walked outside and smelled the cold. The outdoor thermometer anchored on the side of the porch post read thirteen-degrees above zero. The Hinkle sisters had died on a frigid day like this. As I sat on a chipped, faded green kitchen chair outside the doorway, I unexpectedly thought of that last day. I considered the remains of hardened oatmeal in bowls. They used the last of the cut wood; not a stick left anywhere. It was not too long before, Carl Fenster had notified them that he would not be plowing their fields any longer. They would lose that income. Did that help to sway a decision? Physically they were all on the decline. Maybe, the fear of disability loomed large. Violet may have sat her two younger sisters down for a last talk.

My intellect jumped from one thing to another—Amy and the twins, the Hinkle women and their final episode. Who says death is final? Not for the living.

I glanced up at the dismal sky. It had been gray ever since I arrived. It looked like it was about to snow again.

I thought of my talk yesterday with the spectral Thomas Maas. He was resolute about my being stuck in this hill country if it snowed—and quick to admonish.

"A nice lady like yerself, shouldna come alone," he had said.

I assured him I was quite competent and adaptable, and that I didn't come with fears.

"Well, nobody's gonna hurt ya, but what the Sam Hill are ya lookin' for? Seems like everythin's been said." In spite of his words, Maas appeared curious about my findings.

He was a strange, sad man; his face showed the rutted roads of his life. The only living child of seven. Never married. Always there to take care of his widowed mother, Elsa. Lost at love with his soft spot for Lily Hinkle. Worked the mines, but was also a dedicated volunteer fireman and rescuer. Nell, the preacher's wife, recalled how he found the drowned children. Everyone in this community appeared linked to each other. I asked Maas if he would tell me more on the subject of the Hinkle and the Schoen families.

"What? The Schoens? Well, I suppose you heard about Albert's family, isn't that right? Looks like you're writin' about everybody."

I expressed regret if it seemed like I was delving into the community's private matters.

"I guess it's not a secret what happened—but what happened, happened, and that was a long time ago." Maas inhaled deeply on his cigarette, and then crossed his arms tightly over his sunken chest. "I bet you can go to each of these houses in this patch and find sorrow. 'Tain't nobody not touched." He tried to stifle the cough that lived within him. "I'm sure you can look into your own life and see skunks in the woodshed. Ain't that right, Miz Valente?"

I agreed. He was protective of his small society. I replied that since I'd been here, I'd experienced many similar feelings and remembered many poignant situations of my own. I asked him if he thought I should leave, that maybe I had upset people unnecessarily.

"Well, now, there's no need for that. I was just gettin' some steam outta my pipes. I just don't wanta see nobody else hurt."

I assured him, again, that was not my intention.

"The Hinkle girls were the few who were kind to Amy Schoen after them babies died. You could see from the banks, those little ones stuck together under that bridge. It was hard goin' down under to bring them up, don'tcha know. Mighty damn sad. Damn sad. Nobody wanted to talk to that poor girl. It was like she was cursed."

I asked him if anyone had tried to find out the truth.

"Well, hell, nobody asked!" Thomas said, and then spit on the ground. "People just started chatterin' afore they knew anythin'—fillin' poor Albert's head. Had him spinnin'."

My temples throbbed and my nostrils tightened with the stream of cold air. Now I understood wind chill. I returned indoors and walked back to the small writing table, removed my gloves and began probing through bits and pieces of notes. I remembered what Maas had said about the Hinkle sisters befriending Amy. Daisy kept a keen eye on her surrounding neighbors' interactions. It felt as if she were searching, like myself, for the truth of heart matters.

I stopped when I came across Amy's name in one of Daisy's diaries, the year written on the back cover was *1952*.

Amy and Daisy had become worthy confidants. Albert had recommended that his wife speak to the Reverend Miller for guidance, but Amy refused to go. Daisy wrote that she listened carefully to Amy's side of that horrific incident. Without really saying, I gathered her version of the story was different from what the villagers seemed to be saying. Daisy was a persistent patron of integrity. I could understand better why she was so determined in her demands for fairness in the mines. In all of this, I wondered how Lily, Daisy's youngest sister, dealt with the fact of Albert's marriage and losses. It was noted that soon after the tragedy, Lily left Pine Grove Haven.

This family puzzle was growing. Something was up with Lily. And Rose, my goodness, Rose *"Why didn't you fight back, sweetheart—you just couldn't do it. Could you?*

How did Lily feel about Daisy befriending Amy? Did the sisters argue? Was there jealousy or just capitulation? I wanted to know it all. I needed to come back and read this diary more thoroughly.

The winter day was ending. Without electricity, it was impossible to continue, and my eyes smarted with strain. I placed the diary, with the carefully handwritten number *1952* on the lower back cover, on the table.

I got up to stretch. My neck ached. My legs were so cold they would not move quickly. Tonight, I was to have dinner with Thomas Maas and his mother, Elsa. I was a little fearful. If she was as strong as I had heard, I could expect an absorbing evening topped with a wholesome fare, or a case of indigestion.

# *Excerpts from the Diaries of Miss Daisy Maude Hinkle*

**1946—June**

Albert Schoen's out of the Army. He married Amy Bronson last Saturday. Amy has always been an unsettled girl, but they look happy. Her family didn't deserve her. They kicked her around like an old shoe. I'm glad Albert will take care of her now. I know our Lily feels bad since losing Albert, but she's strong. I think she will do all right. She doesn't want to talk about it. She seems restless.

•

**1949—October**

Ma is having some funny pains lately. Maybe it's her rheumatism. I don't think I've ever seen her laugh or smile much.

We have to put up our vegetables. Always enough work to go around. We're starting to get some chilly nights now. Ma still takes care of her folks—enough work, enough work. Ma never talks about our Pa.

•

**1950—May**

We heard that old Mr. Houston, at the garage, got himself a down-and-out-gal to help in the store. She cooks and cleans for him, too. They both can use the help.

Her name is Fannie. He said she could stay with her four kids in the apartment over the garage. They say she was living with them in her car. Always hardship no matter which way you turn. Fannie seems to be a right woman.

He needs the help and she does too. She's been trying to get on the mine payroll, but they're giving her a mean time. They still play those miserable games with women. We have a ways to go.

# *Chapter 7*
# *The Women*

Snow started falling as I came back to the motel. I needed to get warm. It seemed as if the coldness in my body came from deep within. I showered, letting the hot water pound my back.

How often, when I was young, I wished for showers with hot water running freely from the faucet head. Mom and I boiled water on the stove and toted it to the tub, because Dad wouldn't turn on the hot water. I had loathed those brainless restrictions. There was money. There was money for Dad and his luxuries—new cars to show off, an ample supply of exotic and special food, but only when guests were being entertained. I detested the imposed scarcities. We were made to keep up illusions of success and affluence. It was the old refrain—living a lie.

Maybe, it is better to live one's life without churning waters, scrutinizing every point as I often did. But the many layers of these people's existence haunted me. I was tied to them somehow. Why had I been drawn here? The question remained in my head. As little as I believed in the supernatural and the hereafter, there were times during this investigative journey I felt that I had been here before and understood more than I should have.

I stepped out of the moldy and dark concrete shower to towel off. The image of my scarred, dropped-by-gravity-body always shook me. Memories of a smooth and shapely figure seemed to frequently lock to the time before children. The time before caesareans and the surgeon's knives used my belly for a practice playing field, leaving twisted rope-like roads in their wake. The disfigurement embarrassed me. It had been even difficult to let my husband look at me.

But, I didn't have anyone to look at my body, anymore… those days were over.

Suddenly, my mother's voice rang in my ears:

*"Bruta Putanna. You little tramp! You're trying to steal my husband aren't you?"*

*"But, Momma, Momma, Momma! I'm just a little girl and he's my daddy. Momma, don't say those things."*

Why now? Where is this all coming from? *Momma, Momma, what made you so jealous? Why did you resent me for my dad loving me? You acted like a child yourself. When I needed help you weren't there!* I crawled to the bed and moved into a fetal position for ten minutes—wishing the thoughts would go away. My head felt like a carnival act with a three-ring performance in progress. I was getting too enmeshed with these damn diaries. Time to stop thinking about it.

•

That afternoon, I slipped into the comfortable navy chenille top and wool slacks. Tonight I was to dine with Thomas and his mother, Elsa Maas. I put together my gift for them—packages of teas and a tea cozy in tissue. My wool jacket was getting a workout.

It was four-thirty. I stopped to see if Etta Mae had received any messages for me.

"Ain't not a one, Miz Valente," she answered back. "How's it goin'? Findin' you way 'round these hills?"

We chatted about the land and the difficulties surrounding the mining industry. I asked her when she had come to Pine Grove Haven.

"I'd say 'round the 50's. Me an' my Ben used to work in that eastern Kentucky mine. But they lay me off. Women din't have seniority. Terrible times. People gittin' beat-up left and right. That's when we came up here and my man gots him a job in the hole. My kin hepped with the childrun. Afer awhile I gots me one down there, too, we worked different shifts, hardly ever saw ma sweetplum."

Etta Mae leaned over her desk and passed a critical eye over me.

"Dem guys din't much like us women in the mines. A'feared we bring 'em bad luck. Din't want us to get our rightful pay for bustin' our backs. Took some time. But us gals stuck together."

I remembered reading an article about the early seventies; American women began entering coalmines to claim high-wage mining jobs. They dared old superstitions held by male coalminers, who believed that women's presence underground would bring them bad luck and disaster.

"Ben and me put every penny we could in savin's. We was gonna buy us a farm ta raise the young'uns, but Ben din't make it after his accident."

I asked her how she managed to continue.

"Donno. Never had much time ta think about it."

Etta Mae drew back as if shutting down. I told her I had to go because I was visiting the Maas' house for dinner.

"*Ooooeeee!* Maybe, ya could use a prayer meetin'. Ya never know how deep that snake pit is!"

I smiled weakly, raised my eyes, and thanked her for her blessing.

She laughed loud and slapped the desk. "You is good stock!"

I had a sense I was going to run into more weather than I wanted. There was still time to put chains on my tires at the mechanic shop. On the way to the Maas house, I would pass the general market and car repair. It was close to the deserted and ramshackle mine company store.

I slowed to look at a row of tired, vacant shacks. What stories, I speculated, were hidden behind the clapboard sidings? Were there ever any children that laughed and played on similar slate-colored snowdrifts as these?

The two-lane road angled around a broken snow fence. I looked from side to side studying the landscape and imagined what it might look like in summer. I didn't think there would be an improvement. Many of us don't have the luxury to pick where we live. Sometimes we settle for a place because our parents landed there and we think we must stay until we die.

I came to the front of Gottschalt's gas station. As I got out of my car, I noticed that the windows and the sides of the old building were covered in every commercial sign that salesmen could leave. I opened the steamed glass door—the bell at the top announced me.

"Hiya, Miz. Valente," said a dowdy, medium-tall woman.

She stood behind the glass showcase filled with chewing tobacco, cigarettes, antacids, and other miscellaneous sundries. She was one of those women who had decided to forget her looks. I could see under the drab clothing the outlines of a well-formed body.

I was surprised she knew me, but quickly remembered how proficient information worked in this town. She wore wool gloves with the fingers cut out. One of her eyes was dead. Four missing teeth punctuated her smile.

"Findin' your way around?" she asked, her voice coated by years of nicotine.

I thanked her for her concern.

"What kin I do for you?"

I told her I needed help with my chains and asked if she would also fill the gas tank.

She rasped, "Frank, Jr., come out here and help Miz Valente."

Frank, Jr., his head cocked to the side, walked slowly in from the garage. He was a duplicate of his mother in stature and countenance. He wore an unwashed, oil-infused coverall, three sizes larger than his body. Nails were a little ripe from years of car grease, but his smile was pleasant and easy.

"Frank, Jr., put Miz Valente's car chains on and fill that tank. Cars take a beatin' in this kind of cold, don'tcha know. Do you have enough anti-freeze? Check that anti-freeze, Frank, Jr."

We chatted while the car was being serviced. I told her a little about myself. I asked her name.

"Fannie. Fannie Gottschalt."

She spoke openly. Fannie knew all about me, so it seemed. She didn't hesitate to answer my inquiries, making sure she always had a lit cigarette. There were a few tables and chairs set up near the steamy windows for quick coffee, fresh doughnuts, and ready-made sandwiches. A gray tabby took up residence on her own-pillowed chair.

"Yup! After Frank Sr. up and died from his sick lungs, I had to hustle to make ends meet for me and the children. You'll find people here nice enough on the surface, but a little scarce, at first, on spittin' out the whole truth."

I asked why she believed that.

"Don'tcha know that nobody likes to admit they got dirty linen? I guess because we think we should have our crap together, if you know what I mean. Nobody likes to think they're not doin' fine. They're always a few folks with nothin' better to do than point fingers. They get their jollies off by gettin' part of a story and runnin' with it. I just don't like that one damn bit!"

I heard her annoyance and asked if wagging tongues had injured her.

"You betcha! After my mister died, I had to find any work I could. I tried to get work in the mines, but their daddies and granddaddies fought for this seniority system and people thought I was taking a job away from the men. Hell, we had to live, too, but when your mind is made up there's no changin' for some."

Again, I recalled the piece I read regarding the bittersweet memories of the few women who were allowed into the mines around 1973. Accounts of all the times the boss had pitted the miners against them, asking the men how they could let a woman outwork them.

"In many minin' towns, especially in southern West Virginia, there wasn't work above ground and barely any below." Fannie leaned forward with the animated details, "Well, I upped and went to the next town and made good money in tips as a bartender. My four kids and I slept in the car for a couple a months until I saved enough. We ate leftovers, half-eaten bar sandwiches. I saved every penny I could. I come back to try and get a job from ole man Houston. This was his business; he was tryin' to keep it goin'. He was a kind ole sort. Gave me and my family quarters over the auto shop. In turn, I ran the shop and gas station for him. Cooked and took care of him when he got laid up. He left this place to me when he got sick and died. That was a long while back. That was the most anyone has ever done for me. I'll never forget it. Never."

I complimented her for her efforts. She seemed to have an up-front handle on the affairs of the town. I bent to rub the tabby; and the cat immediately turned over on her back to also get a belly pat.

"Yeah, well, thanks, but ya see, not every thing is good. Sometimes stuff happens to people and it ain't too fine." She nodded at the cat. "That's Minnie. I named her that because she reminded me of my mother-in-law, a fine woman. Sure could use her around, but Minnie will have to do. She's a good baby. But as I was saying, just like that poor Amy Schoen, you probably heard about her, after going through such heartache. It ain't right. This town killed her. Mostly them church-going, better-than-you hypocrites."

I looked at her reddening face. Her passion came from a wretched part of her being. Frank, Jr. strode into the store and announced my car was ready. I paid Fannie and told her I'd drop in again soon and spend some time with her.

"You do that. It would be nice. Well, now, you bundle up and watch that road. Where are you headin'? Oh? That's right. Ole lady Elsa Maas? Now there's a winner for you."

## *Excerpts from the Diaries of Miss Daisy Maude Hinkle*

**1950—October**

Albert and Amy Schoen's twins are sweet little things—just turned three. They have the whole world ahead of them. I love to watch them laugh and play. Every time I see them they remind me of Rose and Zachary. There are not enough tears to express our loss. It was the most helpless feeling I've ever had when Zachary died. It changed our family instantly.

It's good the Schoens are fine parents to their babes.

Leaves are starting to turn.

•

**1951—May**

I look and wonder at that young pastor's wife, Nell. Pastor Miller is so loud and hardly allows her to speak. Folks say he's mighty difficult. Reverend Miller seems a little full of himself, but I'm sure I just don't know him yet. Mrs. Miller is a kind sort—but appears a little afraid.

Why is it we consent so often to have others have their say over our lives? She's going to have another baby in September. Her third. I do hope this one lives. It's so awful. I wonder why she loses those children. I've been meaning to spend some time with her, but I don't want to interfere or make things worse. She looks like she could use a friend. It's very hard to get past Pastor Miller. He seems to guard her.

•

**1951—August**

Elsa Maas worked hard to save the pastor's baby, but the little thing was long gone before she came out. Nell sure doesn't have any luck with her babies.

•

**1951—September**

Ma doesn't seem to understand that what Pa did to Rose was evil. We thought that once Pa died she would talk about these incidents. She won't allow us even to speak about these matters. Violet and I have tried to ask questions, but Ma turns a deaf ear, like it never happened. She says, "You mustn't speak ill of your father!"

Ugly things. Just ugly. It's bad enough when strangers do evil things to women and children, but when it's your own pa—I can hardly stand the shame of it. Sometimes I feel like such a helpless and unheard child around Ma.

# Chapter 8
# The Widow Elsa

The driving force of the wind and snow had me troubled.

I dredged up the time my father slid out of control on an icy patch of street and ended up slammed against a light pole, scaring us half to death. His reaction was typical. He screamed at my mother and me because we were frightened, more concerned for his new Buick.

My windshield wipers resisted to keep moving. I drove past Pine Grove Haven Church, past a barn with a farmer struggling to take in the last of his herd of cows.

The weathered, one-story Maas house came into view.

Thomas Maas stood on the front wood landing waiting to greet me. His customary cigarette dangled from his mouth.

"Com'on in. Stomp your feet, will ya. We've been waitin'." He motioned to me to take my coat off and he hung it on the hall tree. The house reeked of years of foul tobacco smoke. I asked if I were late. Thomas ran his hand across his eyes and said I wasn't. I could feel the tightness in this house. He led me directly into the large family-style kitchen. Elsa, his elderly mother, a tight, churlish woman, probably in her middle nineties, sat in a rocker near the potbellied stove, crocheting. She never looked up and didn't acknowledge me when I greeted her.

"Well, now, Ma, our company is here," Thomas's tone was cautious, but loud so that she could hear. He seemed much more constrained than when I first met him at the church hall. "You know, this is the lady who's writin' a story on the Hinkle girls. Her name is Miz Carmela Valente."

"You ain't married?" she shot at me.

I told her I was widowed.

"*Humph!* Women are too free to roam these days. They should be tendin' to family things. The Lord don't take to this kind of out-on-your-own behavior. I smell toilet water."

She finally looked at me, over the wire-rimmed glasses resting on her bony-nose. "I see you wear makeup, too. Makeup is what brought in evil. Must be you're lookin' for a man!"

It was apparent I was in for a tense evening.

"Thomas, are you ready with my dinner?" she demanded.

Thomas gingerly replied, "Yes, Ma. You can come right here now and sit down."

She moved slowly, her hunched back cast a shadow. Her son told me to sit at the table set for the three of us. I looked at him moving about the kitchen. He was gaunt. The years of coal dust and cigarettes were eating away at this man. He put his cigarette down at the edge of the already burnt counter and pulled a shepherd's pie out of the wood-burning stove's oven.

The fragrant aroma drifted into my nose. I asked Thomas if he was generally the cook. I noticed the sour grimace on Elsa's face as she prepared to answer.

"He don't mind cookin'. He keeps things goin'. Feeds the chickens and hogs. He's a good boy. Worked the mines with his father, brothers, and uncles. Was a firefighter, too. Everyone's gone 'ceptin' us." She exhaled noisily. "We don't take to snoopers."

This was not to be a give-and-take conversation. My answers were guarded. I had to find a way to approach this matriarchal force.

For a few moments, except for a leaking faucet, there was complete silence as the serving dishes were passed. The food was wholesome, but lacked color.

"You drink milk?" she inquired. "We have coffee." And before I could answer. "Thomas pour the lady that coffee!"

Thomas Maas jumped up and brought over the blue enamel coffee pot. It had seen better days. The home-canned green beans were overcooked to a gray. The whole house felt and looked gray, like the rest of the valley.

"Whataya think you'll learn about them Hinkles?" she snapped. Her weathered wrinkled face hardly changed, even with her harsh manner.

I told her that I was absorbed with the idea that three old women had made a decision to remain unmarried, to live together as recluses most of their lives, and then, to make a choice to end their lives. I asked if she didn't find that unusual and did she know them well.

"Sure, I knowed them. We women had a tough row-to-hoe. There were days there were hardly any of our men on top the soil. We had to scrape and do the best we could. Babies didn't stop comin'. Mouths needed food. Didn't surprise me them

Hinkles wrapped themselves together." With each sentence Elsa adjusted her clothing as she spoke. The lines on her face appeared to straighten.

I sat back in my chair and knew this would be a rich evening. I asked her if she understood what their life was about.

"What is any life about?" Elsa Maas retorted. "You just plant one foot in front of the other and decide along the way how to get to the end. Some days, it's harder to put that foot down, but ya gotta. It's not about thinkin', it's about doin'. Them Hinkles had their crosses to bear, just like the rest of us. If you stay close to the Bible and to the Lord, he'll show ya the way. Their papa, Sam, was a heathen—didn't want the family to know the Lord. The Lord takes care of us. That's why they had troubles. Sam has probably gone to hell and is burning up. Just like that Amy Schoen. After that Amy died, that Albert fella upped and left his entire family to do Lord knows what in that evil big city. That good for nothin' Clive Mooney is walkin' right beside the devil too! You got daughters?" she asked abruptly.

I answered yes.

"I wouldn't trust him with no daughter o'mine. It don't matter what age they is. He's gonna need some heavy explainin' when he meets the Lord."

"Now, Ma, don't go sayin' things like that. That's not kind. You got to give folks a chance, Clive's a hard worker." her son said as he smoked and ate at the same time.

"Mind how ya talk, Thomas."

I was stimulated by the conversation. It wasn't restrained. I decided to ask her why her life was filled with turmoil. Did she feel that she fared better than the Hinkles because she was religious?

"*Humph.* Now, don'tcha know the Lord did see me

through. My times were hard. I lost most of my family, only Thomas left, but I always had the Bible." She dusted imaginary lint off her lap. "I was always strict with my boys. Mr. Maas worked hard, even though he drank shine. Got a little unruly. But those boys didn't stray."

I asked if any of them married.

"No. No. No," she bellowed. "Most women are evil. Set to destroy men. And men are blinded and lose all sense of their place when they get around skirts. Thomas, here, had his hat set fer Lily Hinkle. But I weren't gonna have any o' that. Things weren't good in that house—they didn't follow the Lord's laws in that house. Anyways, that Sam Hinkle didn't want his girls to meander. My boys were better off. They was good boys."

I wondered why Thomas had asked me to their home for dinner. He surely knew the rancor that filled the walls of this house. I felt sad for him—so taken over by this cynical old woman. She probably demanded, out of her own fears that her children and husband stay on her prescribed path. Maybe, Thomas felt he had so little to lose in asserting my friendship. He was a likeable man, though cheerless.

Her authoritarian manner was seductive. I was seized by her style. In my earlier life, I had easily surrendered the reins to demanding, controlling people. Elsa was triggering that old behavior. Strangely, I enjoyed her. I had a sense that behind all the puffing and moralization, there was another Elsa Maas.

As she ate her supper, Elsa continued her harangue, "Even that Preacher Miller needs some tamin'. Has a wanderin' eye. But that thick-headed wife must enjoy mistreatment. No man would treat me that way. I'd give him some good reasons to cover his skull."

"I've made a peach cobbler," Thomas announced. As he

spoke to me, he kept a heedful eye on his mother. "Can I cut you a piece, Miz Valente? Now don't worry, Ma, I have the crusty, edge piece right here for you."

I was struck by her last comment. Elsa Maas was blowing like Vesuvius, spewing her hot magma of words on whomever she chose to attack, and sometimes contradicting herself. I wondered at what point in her growing up and maturing had Ms. Elsa Maas made a change in her thinking? Or had she always been tight, suspicious, and fearful? I asked her why she said that about Pastor Cyrus Miller.

"What?" she shrieked back. "That man's a cagey sort. Playing with the Lord's collar! Faugh! That wife should've straightened him out long time ago. But she's too mealy mouth to take care o' business. I think she secretly enjoys that man's bullyin'. That's when I decided I didn't need his brand of the Lord's word."

Elsa finished her dessert and slowly returned her stooped hunchback-body to her rocking chair. The pillows were matted down to her shape.

"Ma, don't fill Miz Valente's head up with all that stuff." He turned to me, humiliation in his eyes. "Ma don't have all the facts, Miz Valente."

"Now, ya mind yerself, mister." Elsa raised her crochet hook to a striking position. "I'll not take sassin' from no child o'mine. I kin still whoop your hide."

*Whooping hides.* I thought of all the times my father chose to reason with my mother and me with his fist. How well I knew all the fear that had built up from living with threats. How well I knew those so-called 'loving hands' that turned into tools of domination. The Elsas of the world come in both genders.

"Are you like a reporter?" Elsa grimaced.

I started to answer but she cut me off.

"Could be you're the kind that writes them books that tell all about folks; makin' up what you can't find out? Is that what ya are?"

I attempted to bring her back to the discussion of getting to know her and the Hinkles. She insisted on leading the interview.

"Thomas! Fetch me the picture album."

Her son turned, coughed, and left without a word. In a few minutes he returned carrying a thick book.

"Bring it right here, now." He placed the album in her lap. "I have one of the last pictures of them Hinkle girls. A coupla years back, this man come to town. Said he was an artist. Guessin' he wanted local color. He made drawins' from pictures he took."

I had not seen a photo anywhere of the older Hinkle women. How in all this searching had I not found their faces? I was excited with the prospect of seeing them. Elsa thumbed through the album. In the back of the book, loosely placed, she found a sketch.

"Here 'tis. A good likeness. Not bad for a drawin'. The artist stuck a bonnet on Rose's head. That's Violet, the older girl on yer right. We was young girls together. Tryin' to learn how life was gonna work. She was always tryin' to fix that family. Steered the forces. Kept things in line. Her mother, Lucille, was always stealin' her thunder. She couldn't stand the fact that Sam liked his daughters. He liked them a little too much, I would say. Lucille wouldn't stick-up for them gals...no matter what. Daisy's in the middle. Tall like her father. She liked to write and raise grief with the miners. She was pretty good with people. Seemed to know how to talk and soothe folks. We usta call her 'Sista Daisy'. Ha!"

Her recollections of the Hinkle women were at times contradictory.

"And there's Rose on the left. She were a good girl. Taught the miners and their families to read and write...later seemed to back off from life." Elsa's deformed arthritic finger pointed to the picture as she talked. "Violet said that Rose was havin' a hard time with things. I'll bet she was—had enough to feel bad about. Caught her cryin' out back of the barn one time. Someone shoulda taken that Pa of hers and put one between his eyes. Rose was in her own head most times. That young'un Lily's not here 'cause she went off on her own. Independent hussy. Left her sisters to fend for themselves."

I took the artist's sketch in my hand. There was an overall sweetness and reflective quality in the three aged women. Their slender bodies leaned towards each other, heads close. Shivers ran up my spine as their deep-set, crater eyes reached into me. Daisy's doleful and limpid round ones spoke to me the loudest. I could feel her stare. Their faces showed the years; fissures in their foreheads; clamped thin-lipped smiles set. Leathery faces framed by silver hair parted in the center and pulled back to the nape of their neck. Their aquiline noses added distinction.

Violet, wearing an initialed brooch and steel-rimmed spectacles on her fuller face, was the shortest. It was as if she wanted to speak. Rose wore a bonnet to the back of her longer-shaped head. She appeared the more distant as if looking away from the artist.

I was delighted with the humanness of the sketch. It looked like they were peering out of an oval-shaped picture frame.

"They was good girls, but they needed the Lord to help em! Their mother, Lucille, I suppose, was a good 'nough mother, but didn't stick-up for them 'nough to suit me. Seemed a bit jealous of her girls."

As I listened to Elsa going off on the way children and young women should be raised, her voice fading in and out, I was absorbed with the view of Violet, Daisy, and Rose. They looked older than I imagined. The picture cemented the reality of the women's lives.

I wanted to ask more questions of Elsa. I decided just to let the conversation flow, even though her harshness disturbed me.

"I been round here a long time, and I seen it all. Nobody kin put anythin' over on ole Elsa. People can't fool me, I tell you. Their daddy was a rounder. Could steal the gold right from your teeth as you're smilin'."

"Ma, now Mr. Hinkle was a honest man," Thomas quickly defended. "Why are you saying such things? He worked hard to keep his family." Thomas turned towards me. "We all worked hard, Miz Valente. No one got away with too much. There is always a few bad apples."

I nodded in agreement.

"Yep," Elsa interjected. "Don't think you knowed everythin', Thomas J. Maas. You don't knowed everythin'" Her voice dropped and she looked off to the ceiling. Silence and then she picked up speed again, "Like that tobaccy-chawin' reverend. He is busy spreadin' wickedness as he speaks the Lord's words. I understand you had supper with him and Nell. Whatcha know bout him?"

I confirmed my visit to the Millers', but I wanted to hear Elsa's views on things, especially the Schoen drowning. I was fearful of not being able to keep the comments from getting out of hand. I had already heard her bias towards Amy Schoen.

"Well, Lord knows it were one bad day. My Thomas took

those dead babies out from under that Stoneman Bridge. One bad day. They was holdin' hands. Awful day. Their ma was too busy. Too busy to watch them children."

I stood up and looked down at Elsa. I couldn't contain my opinion any longer. I took Pine Grove Haven's memories personally. She knew I was annoyed.

"Somethin' wrong?" she said, straining her neck to look at my face. "You look kind of rosy."

I asked her why she felt she could be so overly critical of a situation about which she had only hearsay information. Where was the solid evidence that Amy Schoen did something so foul as to allow her children to die? This story was alive and kicking after all these years. What was going on in this town? Why was this truth being compromised?

"Well, now," Elsa responded, "I should know somethin' since I brung those babes into the world and, young girl, I would say you need a lesson in mindin' your manners. Our yarns are none of your concern."

I apologized for losing my temper. I explained the different versions I had heard of the very sad story. Her demeanor relaxed. Her myopic eyes narrowed. I guessed not many had dared to speak back to Mrs. Elsa Maas.

I thought of all the conversations I was party to in my lifetime, dialogues that had allowed the escape of opportunities to rectify wrongs, chances to change strong dictatorial minds with logic and accuracy. Why do we, as people, buckle so easily to these sharp tongues?

The notion of finding out how her character evolved attracted me. I had an idea that I could challenge her with the right approach.

Thomas looked haggard. He nodded. "Can I get you anythin' else, Miz Valente?"

Elsa answered her grown son, "Not now, Thomas, I want to talk to this young woman. Just bring her more coffee."

I thanked her for the 'young woman' compliment. She gave me her first grin, and then fired off questions about my upbringing and personal history. I had always been the one who could control conversations and steer them away from my past. I told Elsa Maas that these questions made me a little uncomfortable. I told her of the expectations of living in a home of an immigrant, who felt compelled to succeed and to have total control over his wife and family. I was even able to tell her how much my sister and I were affected by the loss of our little sister.

"Losing children is like having a carving knife anchored to your heart. Everytime you move it cuts in a little deeper." She glared at me. "I suppose you got some of that higher learnin'."

I nodded and answered yes.

"When I was a young girl," Elsa said, "I asked my ma 'n pa if I could go to school like my brothers, but they said girls don't need educatin'. I wanted to read like the boys, so when they did their studies at night, I listened. It were a different life in them days. No time to fritter an' fret." As I listened to her free range of opinions and beliefs, I detected a tone-down of her crusty attitude. We spoke for nearly an hour-and-a-half. I continued to wonder if there wasn't more in the woman's life that brought her to this edge. I asked Thomas if he remembered growing up with his parents, especially his mother.

"Yup. Ma worked hard. In between raisin' all us boys, she were a *granny woman*. I spent many a night runnin' with her to help some poor mother and her new babe." Thomas looked proudly at his mother.

"Now, Thomas that were a long time ago. Miz Valente don't want to hear 'bout that. Only the Lord knows how much misery we seen in those days. *Mmmhuh."*

I had never heard that phrase before for a midwife. I asked Elsa why and how she learned about this part of medicine.

"Didn't have a choice," Elsa said. "I had to help my ma with my younger brothers. Ma was alone in the potato patch when she started yellin' for me. I was eight. I helped her to the house, and she told me what to do. The two of us brought the little mister to the world. I had to cut the cord and wipe the little thing."

*"I know, Momma. I know, Momma. You always tell me how you almost died having me. But what can I do about it? I'm sorry, Momma. You're sorry I was born aren't you?"*

Why had that popped into my head? It was an old hurt, and I'd dealt with it long ago.

I couldn't get over how different conversations with these folks kept triggering old wounds with my father and mother. It felt like the eruption of a dormant volcano. This journey was taking me into dark caverns of my soul.

Elsa continued, "After that, it seemed I was always 'round when others needed my ma, and I went along. Just like Thomas. Sure no way to come easy into this world. We come in screamin' an' hollerin' and some of us leave the same way. I just about cleaned every backside in this here valley, and many I helped to bury."

I told her how sad I felt for Nell Miller, the pastor's wife, having lost five children. She seemed like such a fine woman. I asked Elsa if she had assisted Nell with the births.

"Yep," she answered curtly, her lips tightly pursed again. "Some things is best left to the Lord to sort out. That man didn't want her to have them children."

Elsa was lost in thought for a moment. I drew back also, astonished at her statement.

"I think it's gettin' close to my bedtime, now. Thomas, you help Miz Valente with her coat 'n overshoes. I thank ya for the nice cotton hand towels. It's been fine talkin' to ya. I 'spect we'll be seein' ya agin' afore ya leave."

The abrupt end to our conversation amazed me. Something changed and didn't sit right with Elsa. Maybe, she felt she had been too disclosing. I glanced at Thomas' awkward face. I bid his mother good night and thanked her for her hospitality. Thomas assisted me with my jacket, snowshoes, and scarf. As I put on my knit cap and gloves, I reflected on how peculiar the evening had turned out.

Suddenly, I felt a hurried need to get back to the safety of my room. That strange aloneness had a way of creeping into my psyche. The feeling that I was at the edge of a high window—teetering on the sill and no one there to prevent me from falling.

*"What are you afraid of, Carmela? All you have to do is take care of the baby. There's no bogeymen in there! Gowan! Don't be a big baby! Momma and daddy are coming back. Maybe."*

Thomas opened the rustic door and searched my face as if he wanted to say something more than the social closure. I smiled and thanked him again for his generous meal. He seemed pleased when I told him I decided to extend my stay in Pine Grove Haven, and I looked forward to our meeting again in the next few days.

As I stood on the small porch, I looked at the snow and hoped I wouldn't encounter problems with the road trip back to *Etta Mae's Drift On Inn Motel.* A light sprinkling of flakes had been falling steadily throughout most of the crisp evening. That certain stillness in a winter's night reminded me of my youth.

"Don't pay no mind to Ma, Miz Valente," Thomas said, trying to hide his gap-tooth smile. He extended his coarse hand to shake mine.

"She likes you."

## *Excerpts from the Diaries of Miss Daisy Maude Hinkle*

**1952—April 30**

Wretchedness made its stop here again. Tragedy never stops. Death seems to be comfortable here. This day will never be forgotten. My God, those babies!

Thomas Maas tried to rescue the Schoen babies from Black Creek. Poor Amy, she's so fragile and Albert was so proud of his little family. They will suffer forever.

Already ugly rumors are flying. People don't know what to do with their fears.

•

## They Was Holdin' Hands

**1952—June**

I loved the creek when I was small and I couldn't resist the temptation. Children are always drawn to water.

Old man Schoen said he planned to put up a fence around Albert's house to protect the grandchildren, but never got around to it. There is always a large supply of guilt to be had.

The miracle is that more of us weren't swallowed up by Black Creek. That water rushes something fierce in spring. So beautiful, yet deadly. Sometimes Mother Earth is downright unfriendly – like she's cleaning house.

I can't even imagine how Thomas felt when he found those babies beneath Stoneman Bridge. I was told he had tears streaming down his face. He said little Glenna Sue and Albert Jr. were nestled together—they were holding hands. They left jointly, just like the day they came.

# Chapter 9
# Fannie Gottschalt's Recollections

The drive down the quiet highway put me in a pensive mood. This community went to bed in the early hours of evening and rose with the chickens, as my aunt would say. It was a little past eight, too soon to go to bed for my style of living. At home, I'd just be coming alive. Late hours were comfortable. But, heck I liked morning time, also. Truth is, sleeping is a nuisance. Cat napping is fun, though. Each morning, unless I had an appointment, I stumbled out of bed, took my AM. meds, then marched to the word processor and spent three or four satisfying hours writing my imagined Pulitzer.

Thoughts kept bouncing in and out of my head. The evening visit perplexed me. Elsa was mellowing, but she buttoned up when I asked about Nell Miller and the children she'd lost.

The town and its tenants reminded me of a tremendous white lace tablecloth—an intricate design, each complete and each spider-webbing into neighbors lives. Every household held mysteries. Unexpectedly my mind jumped to another time. I felt the palpitations in my neck and throat.

*Forget about it! No one needs to know what happened! You're stupid. So what if you thought he was just a friend. You shouldn't have gotten in the car alone with him, playing grown-up games. When are you going to grow up and learn?*

Bastard. I let him get away with it.

*"Hey Carmela, why don't we stop over here at the park. I want to show you what I bought today. It'll just take a minute."*

*"Michael, I have to be at Dr. Penna's office or he'll fire me. I really don't think I should. What are you doing? You're acting weird."*

*"Com'on! I'll tell you when we leave."*

*"You're hurting me!"*

I trusted him. I thought because he was older I could trust him. I trusted my so-call-friend. He cornered me in the car. He made believe he was interested in me. The miserable bastard! I trusted Michael, Dr. Penna's gay friend. I was stunned by the fierceness of his attack. I never told anyone about this rape. Nobody. Nobody would have believed me.

*Michael, you son-of-a-bitch! You fucking son-of-a-bitch! May you rot in hell!*

I pulled the car to the side of the road and leaned my body against the steering wheel. My head felt as if it were in a vise. I couldn't even cry. But I could scream. I wished to hell I had never come to this black hole—why did I need this? Oh, I was learning a lot here—more than I wanted to know.

I needed a cup of coffee or something stronger. I had the shakes.

The lights were still on at Fannie Gottschalt's service station. Her silhouette moved about inside the store. A cup of hot chocolate sounded comforting. I stopped.

"Well, hi!" Fannie shouted, "Isn't this a nice surprise!"

I waved to her, glad to get the warm greeting. I heaved a sigh as I sat at a table and threw down my large purse on the next chair.

"Somethin' wrong? You ain't got color. You're back early from Elsa's. You don't have to tell me. She beat you up? She probably called the shots. Right?"

She laughed when I agreed and brightened at the thought of a conversation. Her worn body belied her engaging personality.

"One thing I know is people! That ole lady's been around a long time and that ole brain has soaked up a hellava lot of information, but she's good—no malarkey with her. What'll ya have, Miz Valente? Coffee? No? Hot cocoa? Yep, I have this machine right here that'll pump out a good cup of hot chocolate. I'll have it in a jiffy."

She brought the steaming beverage to the table and threw down a couple of homemade sugar cookies. Fannie drank strong smelling coffee, probably from the last pot of the day.

"Say you best be careful of running these highways. There's been some ugly things happenin' to women not from this town. They say they gonna catch the puke that's botherin' these gals, but I ain't seen nobody caught yet. You know how that goes. Women don't get main concerns too quick."

Talk about coincidence—there must have been a script posted somewhere around there. I wanted to tell her what I had just been through, but I couldn't quite face it all just yet. I was glad for the warning. I asked her how long she usually stayed open.

"Oh, until about eleven or so because of them truckers. I keep an ear to the C B radio. They let me know when they're gonna come for a bite. They fly through here in those damn eighteen-wheelers like locomotives," she ranted. "Yeah. I make enough to pay the bills at the end of the month. But not much more. I don't see myself retiring any too quick."

Fannie reached down under the counter to get more cartons of cigarettes to place, neatly lined by brand, on the wall behind the register. I asked where her son was.

"Frank, Jr. is studyin'. I wanna help get that man educated. He was workin' for a long time in a goin'-nowhere-job in Harrisburg, then he decided he wanted to come back here to help me. That way he can save some money and get an education. He's getting' a late start, but he'll make it. Then he can leave like my other three. Ain't no gettin anywhere or out of here if you don't get smart. I learnt that pretty quick. He wants to study crime. You know like a forensic guy."

I asked her if her other children were boys or girls.

"What? Oh yeah, I got girls. They moved on. Melissa Ann lives in Philadelphia. Teaches them kids that don't hear. I had my hands full with her not being able to hear, but we made it. Mary Lee, she's married to a good man and has a couple of kids, runs a bed-and-breakfast, a nice place, in the Shenandoah Valley. Kind of a resort area."

Fannie's waving hands and arms punctuated the particulars, as she told of her family. "Robyn Lee, she's a Park Ranger. Right now, she's workin' at the Shenandoah National Park. They all good kids. Come to see me every chance they get. Mary Lee, she's my oldest, wants me to sell the business and come live near her. Now, what do you suppose I'd do out there sittin' on a lawn chair with nobody to talk to? I'm settled here. I know what to expect. No use stirring the pot. She don't like my smokin' anyways. Only problem is, if Frank, Jr. leaves I'll need to get me another mechanic."

I gave her the minutiae of my evening at the Maas'. I told her of seeing a drawing of the Hinkle women and then how it ended with the discussion of Nell Miller and her babies. She leaned toward me, the ash on the cigarette ready to fall into her cup.

I looked at Fannie's bloated visage; a ridge of fuzz lined her lip, a few blackheads nested in her face, and her long-ago-dyed hair ends hung limply on her collar. I wondered what it was that told her to stop caring.

"Well, you sure are gettin' a baptism by fire, ain'tcha?"

I nodded in agreement and told her how I was affected by the news of the community, and not sure if I was stirring the proverbial hornet's nest.

"Now, don't you worry your head. It's nothin' you've done."

She looked pensive for a moment, dragged deep on her cigarette, and then took a sip of coffee.

"I think I know what ole Elsa Maas didn't want to tell you. But hell! I don't know why not? We women are fools for protectin' these heavy-handed men. Them babies didn't stand a chance to come out alive. Elsa saw to all the birthin'."

I listened, appalled at her words.

"The *good preacher* thinks he's above it all. He thinks he's got us all hoodwinked, hidin' behind that righteous pulpit." Fannie leaned back on the bentwood chair, waving her hands as she spoke, "He whooped his woman senseless. Just like a rag-doll."

I sat aghast, listening to the verbal gush.

"Elsa saw the bruises. She gave him hell. He said she just fell down. Fell down my fat foot!"

I was well acquainted with that kind of falling down.

*"Don't hit her Daddy! She's sorry—Aren't you Mommy? Don't*

*say anything, then he won't get mad."*

When I was young, women were taught carefully to be passive and accommodating. We are good at teaching people how to treat us. I looked at the hardness of Fanny's features and guessed a story behind each loss: a sightless eye, missing teeth, an immobile left index finger, a slight limp on her right side. But I admired Fannie's candor and pluckiness.

"I know it took me a long time to learn to stand up for myself," Fannie continued. "There ain't no glory in peace-at-any-price, now is there? That Nell keeps to herself. I don't trust that Cyrus—he ain't worth a dime to me. I think she knows more than she's tellin'. She don't take his guff anymore. After she buried that last one, she seemed to change."

She stood quiet a moment.

"Our cemetery is filled with the other half of our lives. There're just so many cheeks to turn, now ain't there? This face has felt the backside of a hand plenty times. All in the name of love. Now ain't that a bunch of crap? Damn strange way to show how much you care about someone. Most of it happened after Frank Sr. died. He were a good man. Couldn't find another one like him. Ran into a couple of winners that used me like a punchin' bag. I knew I was in for a tough road, with four young ones. I had to do whatever it took to take care of us. Them money trees don't grow in Pine Grove Haven."

I didn't need to question her. She was on automatic. I sat in stoic silence as she opened the sealed memories of hurts, both physical and emotional, that no doubt once bled profusely.

Fannie took my cup to refill the chocolate drink.

"Men beat up on their women when they get scared. You get my meanin'? It's like they have so little themselves. So little control on what they can have or say. Frank, Sr. used to come home from the mines black. Left when it was black, came home when it was black. We celebrated our lives in the dark. The days he woke to sunlight he didn't know what to do—he was scared."

She stopped and looked towards the windows.

"Want a smoke? Maybe a little schnapps?"

I shook my head no. I thought of the fear that must have guided my father's hands. An immigrant with more desires than skills. A man, who left his poverty-stricken parents and siblings to prove he could become the catcher of the brass rings. No one told him of The-Rich-White-Anglo-Saxon-Males that would spread spikes of prejudice in his path and make unending demands on him that smacked of slavery. While he struggled to learn the language, he would do anything to put food on our table, never sure if at the end of the day there would be any approval. He had barely enough power over his life. Yes, he was frightened. Mother was frightened. We were all frightened.

"You're a widow, ain'tcha?" Fannie asked.

She knew the answer.

"Damn lot of widows on this planet. How'd he die? Kidney failure, heh? Always somethin' is gonna get ya. Did you like him?"

I told her I met him when I was seventeen and I knew he loved me. I certainly loved him, but we had our headaches. He was a good provider to our family—fairly good long marriage. He supported me through my parents' mean streaks. I told her that I would probably have gone off the deep end if it hadn't been for him. I was fortunate.

"Good. That's good."

I went on to say how his fears sometimes made for his inflexible ways, which cornered our on-going disagreements.

"Well, I do know stubborn. What kind a work did he do?

Worked with criminals? Well, I got to tell Frank, Jr. about him. *Huh.* Like a policeman? Oh, them head-sick ones. *Huh.* Ain't it strange? I guess we all could be offenders. All it takes is the right situation. Some situations teach you how to forget the law."

Fannie studied my face and lit her fourth cigarette. She fired questions as quick as I could respond. I sat for quite some time revealing data, thoughts, and feelings. I marveled at my openness with this quasi-stranger. Even with my closest friends, I had not shared moments this deep and intimate. Something about this valley drew me to the surface. As Fannie said, other than the stories of Amy Bronson and the Hinkles, there were few false fronts to deal with here. But she supposed they were, in many ways, a guarded community. In the large cities where I lived most of my life, people seemed more careful of the image they gave of themselves, even fabricating their lives to suit the need to fool. A distinct picture was forming of this vale.

A man came in and stomped his feet on the entry mat. He shuddered as he stood in the doorway. He looked at me carefully, tipped his cap, and then softly spoke to Fannie. She walked to the cold case and handed him a six-pack of beer, took his money and patted him on the back.

"See you later, Dewey. Say hello to your pa. He doing okay?"

"Yeah, I guess he doing fine for now. I ain't been home from work yet today. I've been buildin' a big porch in the next county. Pa had a couple of bad days this week. I don't know how long he has. Been spittin' up quite a bit. Sis is worried."

Dewey's answers rolled off easily as he shifted weight on his scrawny frame. A five o'clock shadow outlined his lean, good-looking face.

"When he goes, ain't nobody left 'ceptin' me and her." His tired-looking black eyes drifted upwards. "See ya later, Fannie."

"You come by if ya need help, Dewey. No sense being alone."

"Thank ya, I'll keep that in mind."

There seemed to be a constant need to grieve here. I told her how much I appreciated her company. I felt secure with her. I didn't grow up feeling close to or trusting women. My own mother didn't have the capacity of parenting, especially doling out love. I didn't trust her with my hurts. She'd pulled the rug out from under me too many times. There was a genuine maternal aura about Fannie.

"This here is demandin' country," she said, after Dewey left. "When you're born here, hardships are closer together. Coalminers and their families see the earth from the inside out."

# *Excerpts from the Diaries of Miss Daisy Maude Hinkle*

**1952—July**

It's been a couple of months since the Schoen twins died. The whole community was affected by this tragedy. I long to hear laughter. Someone needs to laugh.

It's very hard to look at that poor girl, Amy. I can't tell how she's doing. I sense she wants to talk to me. Folks are cruel. She needs help. Maybe I'll ask her tomorrow if she wants to speak to Pastor Miller—although I don't care much for him.

•

**1952—November**

Amy is looking terribly haggard. I think she is drinking heavily. I've tried to get her to reason some of this heartbreak but she is so overwhelmed with grief.

It has been seven months since her babies died in Black Creek. I still can't get over what she told me – I wish she had not sworn me to secrecy. I told her I think she should expose the shameful man. She became hysterical when I said that. I dare not break her confidence.

I find it interesting that no one will come right out and say who was pestering her. Amy is so fragile and afraid that Albert will do something reckless. He keeps up a brave front, but I see all of this haunts him. Daily, their misfortune continues to grow.

Amy Schoen is not a strong girl to fight off all that has happened. She needs help. She didn't do anything wrong. I tried to talk to Albert, but he's got his mind made up. He'll kill that wretched man if he catches him.

# *Chapter 10*
# *Deliverance*

I was drawn to spend another day at the Hinkle house. On my drive up the narrow back roads, I decided to check out the community's cemetery. I recollected, when I was young, my mother's relatives spent a fair amount of time in graveyards. My father was the only one in his immediate family that we knew immigrated to the United States—he was in his early twenties. His oldest brother left Sicily for Argentina. In a dramatic argument with his sister, my father chased her out of Sicily. I often wondered what that was all about, or where she went.

On Memorial Day and other holidays, my grandparents came to clean around the family plots and plant new annuals. A few of their children were buried there. Taking care of the dead was as important to them as caring for the living.

What could I learn from visiting this place? I had no particular reason for being there, just a strange energy pulling me. Graveyards have a way of revealing stories. Often I've walked through them wondering whether some of the more elaborate resting places weren't the result of guilt on the part of the living with respect to unfinished matters with the dead.

I drove the rental car through the gates of *The Perpetual Peace Cemetery* and circled the perimeter of the memorial grounds. The sun's glare on my windshield played strange scenes with the gravesites. I stopped in a clearing and began to walk between the markers. The warmth of the sun on my back was comforting.

*"Mommy, what are they going to do with the baby? Why do they have to put Gioia in a box?"*

*"Keep quiet. They're going to put her in the dirt."*

*Gina asked, "Why? Did she do something wrong?"*

I was remembering my sister's funeral. It had always been a missing piece of my life. Why was I remembering it now?

It wasn't our fault! It wasn't our fault! Gina and I did nothing wrong. I couldn't remember what had happened, but it wasn't our fault. We were just little girls, ourselves.

At every turn, I was having to deal with new and old feelings and now new memories of things long past. Turning my attention back to the graves, I observed that an incredible number of men had been struck down at early ages, long before they could taste the swell of life. Often, their monuments were larger than women's—a matter of importance?

Most married women, their maiden names lost and no longer with their birth families, now rested with a surname. Recognition appeared to be of great significance. In spite of this region's scarcity of money, the living felt obliged to pay the tab for eternal elegance.

Cold stone angels sat atop tombstones on watch, waiting

for the next tenants.

I recognized many family names. I finally came across a large unadorned marker belonging to the Hinkle family. Father Sam had the most significant stone. Mother Lucille's was shaped like a heart and inscribed:

*Mother, you tried and you cried,*
*And when you shed enough tears you died.*
*Why did you leave us?*

Nearby rested Zachary, their sixteen-year-old-son.

*Here lies Zachary*
*Although his body be crushed, his courage was never*
*We love you dear brother and son*

And then I saw an impressive headstone for Violet, Daisy, and Rose, the women that drew me to this part of the country. Chiseled into the stone were hands linked together. Below that, three children dancing in a circle, their faces bright with freedom, arms intertwined, heads tossed back. A simple epitaph read:

*They was holdin' hands*

I realized Lily must have had the monument put there. Perhaps, to ease guilt because she had abandoned them in later years.

I brushed away the snow from a concrete bench and sat down. The day was clear. No heavy, bleak clouds blocked the sun's welcome gift. I watched as the melting rivulets of snow slid down the gravestones like tears. I turned and realized I was next to Schoens' burial plot. I stood up and walked towards Amy Bronson Schoen's grave—next to her twins, Albert Jr. and Glenna Sue. Three stone crosses were placed in a decorative, fenced area. Embedded in the middle and largest cross was a photograph of a joyous laughing Amy and her babies. I remained motionless for a moment as I soaked up the enormity of these final images.

Daisy Hinkle befriended this young woman. At some point in their relationship, Amy confided, like daughter to mother, her poignant fears and desires. I've often witnessed people avoiding those who have experienced immense tragedy—fearing the contamination of feelings. Daisy made a difference. That's the most many of us hope to do.

I heard the sound of crunching snow.

Footsteps.

"You certainly do find your way around," a controlled voice said.

I recognized the quality. It was Albert Schoen. I felt self-conscious. There was that awful reaction again of not having a right to peer into these lives. I turned as he approached. His slate eyes seemed transfixed. I detected a change in him. A dreadful veil of sadness covered his worn, handsome face.

"I spend a great deal of time here just sitting on this bench. I'm not sure why." He pressed his full lips together.

I zipped my jacket up to my neck. I sensed he trusted me.

"By now my children would be fully grown with families of their own. I tell myself to get a hold and get over it. But all that is book theory."

Albert moved in a circular pattern pronouncing the discourse with the wave of his right hand. The left hand remained deep in his coat pocket.

"Have you ever lost anyone, Ms. Valente?"

I replied yes, immediately thinking of my dead son and my little sister and of all the people that died that had moved into my heart.

"Women are smart. They form units and encircle their cocoons about the injured one, nourishing and soothing the emotional bleeds. Men aren't taught these lessons. They're not as prepared for internal discomfort from tragic loss."

He paused and looked at me; he seemed to be searching my face for disinterest.

"I am sorry to be going on so. You barely know me. And yet I feel as if I have known you all my life. How perfectly strange."

He left me no opportunity to comment. I reassured him with a smile.

"Sometimes there is no one I can express these God-awful rages to. There are times I do fine, but then there are those days that make mush of my thinking."

I told him his disclosures would be safe with me.

"Somehow, I knew you would say that. I could tell when I met you."

He sat down on the bench and removed his leather gloves. His eyes now looked strained. He took his large, smooth hands and rubbed his face, as if to lift the web of ache that covered it, and then ran his fingers through his silver, wavy hair. His shoulders slumped. I could see this man was truly broken. I had mistaken his brave and calculated facade. I was raised around men, who showed emotion openly. There was none of this repressive make-believe; if there was anguish it was shared frankly.

I glanced at him and put my hand on his drooping back. I told him not to be afraid to tell me anything if it would help him feel better. In my mind, I questioned if it wasn't unusual to linger in grief for so long. After all, it had been many years since that unhappy day. I asked him why he chose to come back to this place of so many sad memories.

With that query the dam burst in Albert Schoen.

"What? Hell, even my family doesn't know what I went through in all these past years. Everyone ignores the big talk. They're so busy keeping up their walls there is no place for any breakdowns. No one has ever asked."

His usually calm voice quavered as he articulated his melancholia.

"People are brainless. Do they ask? Well, Albert, how goes it? Doing all right? How does it feel, Albert, for everyone you love to die? Want fried or mash potatoes, Albert?"

He stood up and turned towards me, but did not look at me. He waved his hands as if he were announcing from a pulpit. I sensed he was barely aware that I was there listening.

"For years, I was like a robot. A damn robot! Push a button, I bow. Push a button, I sleep. Push a button, I talk and eat. Push a button, I performed for the corporation."

His words were clear.

"Finally, after ten years of stone, silent agony, I found a woman who gave me love and kindness and helped me to turn off my idiotic mechanical thinking. We married and had a splendid life in Manhattan. She was a little *avant-garde* and crazy, loved the theater, she taught me to laugh, and I trusted she would always be there when I needed her. I began to believe that maybe I might survive the death of Amy and the twins."

There was a long pause, and then Albert again gazed to the sky. "And as if the past wasn't bad enough, five-years ago, Margo, my new wife, was diagnosed with cancer, an inoperable brain tumor. She died in my arms three months later. I was numb from it all. I decided to run again. This time, to retreat to my hometown, thinking this would give me meaning. But no; there are no answers."

He walked to the grave of his first wife and children and began to pound on Amy's cross.

"Why, why, why?" he shouted. "We were happy. I used to think it was because I didn't show you how much I loved you. I just didn't know how to prove it. My God, I lost everything! You, too, were drowning, and I didn't know how to save you."

The veins in his forehead throbbed with each exclamation.

"You made my life whole and exciting. I loved you with all my being. You didn't need to die! It wasn't your fault! I want to believe that. You were a good mother and the children were your everything. It was an accident. Vicious tongues killed you! But why? I didn't like hearing that some man was in the house that day. I kept asking you, but you wouldn't tell me. Why were you trying to protect him? If it was your cousin, Farley, I would have understood. He was always annoying all the girls. Oh, Amy, how I wish I could live those weeks over again."

Shivers ran through me like darts. I could hear the questions that haunted him. The doubts. Tears he had held back for so many years began flowing down his pitiable face. I walked over to Albert and grasped his broad arms and shoulders from behind. He whimpered and sobbed.

"I'm sorry, Ms. Valente. I thought I was handling things just fine until I started to notice flubs in my decision-making—in my company—with friends and relationships. Then I became mindful of how every thing I touch dies."

I felt inadequate to help this wretched man face these demons of death that had almost pulled him to his own.

I remembered how Dad would scream at Momma in Italian, when he was desperate and out of control: *"Why don't you help me love my children? You see I need help, but you just sit there like a stupid! Don't you care?"*

It is so easy to pass judgment in retrospect. What ever happened to the idea of parents protecting their children? I certainly didn't feel protected. For years, I was mad and disgusted with my parents, especially mother, but now I know that she couldn't support her family. She didn't know how. She had shut down because of my father's abuse. She was a child in so many ways and didn't know how to take care of herself. You can't give away something you don't have.

Mother had also come from wretched rules. There is that vicious chain reaction of life that stretches from one generation to the next. It takes courage to break an unsound system that is so carefully welded in place.

Like it or not, Albert was facing his adversary. After his emotional eruption he began to relax.

"You must think I'm crazy. This is embarrassing," he said, wiping his face and eyes with a handkerchief. "I guess I've held this stuff in for a long time."

I told Albert how hard it was for my husband to deal with the death of our infant son. Oh yes, there were tears. But to really assess what the meaning of his loss was, he had to examine deeper, masked thoughts. For my husband, having a son, our last child, insured by a tubal ligation at the time of the delivery, had special meaning. He was to carry forth his father's name, and with any luck, stem mid-life weariness. But, I also told Albert that our loss could not be compared to his experiences. His were off the scale.

I suggested we get a cup of hot coffee or tea at Fannie Gottschalt's place.

"Yes, that would be good, but, Ms. Valente, I've pressed

too hard on your kindness. I'll be fine now. I don't know what came over me. Sometimes I wonder if there is a God. He must be sitting somewhere out there watching me struggle. The question is why? I think all this unearthing of the past is like raising a relic ship. There's bound to be barnacles."

He straightened and I could see a shift in his composure.

"By now you must be gathering quite a picture of our community" he said, his tone steady and sonorous.

I acknowledged that I was. The interpretation of these people, his friends, I said, was not too different from my own society. People shared what they trusted me to hear. There were those who were cautious, defensive, and thorny, but they seemed to speak for the most part from their hearts. They simply didn't want to be misused or misunderstood.

"Yes," he agreed. "It is important not to be misrepresented."

He took my hand. "Thank you for being fair-minded."

Venera Di Bella Barles

# *Excerpts from the Diaries of Miss Daisy Maude Hinkle*

**1952—November**

Tomorrow is Thanksgiving, and I'll be fifty-one in three days. Seems like I was just twenty-five, and I had my whole life ahead of me.

At least Lily is married and has a fine boy and girl. She doesn't bring them around. She's ashamed of us. I wonder if she will ever learn the truth.

I've sent in two of my short stories to a couple more magazines. Still no luck, I need to find a better way.

It looks like we'll have our first snowfall of the year. It has been so unmercifully chilly. I never get used to this much cold.

Why is it that winter always feels closer to death?

•

**1953—January**

Molly, that works next to me in the mill, got her hand caught in a machine today. They brought in a new woman to take her place. Seems a little slow in the head, but a nice sort. They say she's the only one who is working in her big family. She needs this job bad. She's from the next county. Not married. Everyone has a story.

•

**1953—April**

Amy Schoen's doing hard time without her babies.

It's been one year. She's holed up in her house, barely able to get out of bed. She and Albert seem strained. She's not eating and has been drowning her sorrows in applejack. She can't last long doing that.

Wagging tongues are like mine explosions. You just don't know where the shale will land. Makes everyone run for cover.

# *Chapter 11*
# *Relentless Wisdom*

Clive Mooney's beer delivery truck was parked in front of the general store. As I pulled into the parking lot, I watched Clive come out of Fannie's place. He lit his cigarette and drew in deeply. Then he smiled at me with a stabbing glare as he zipped up his leather jacket. He climbed into the cab of his vehicle, never removing his eyes from me. Those un-named jitters returned. I was relieved when Albert's car drove in and parked next to mine. The horizon was lost in gray.

"Well, what a good thing to see ya." Cold vapor wrapped Fannie's words as she held the frosted plate glass door open for us. At once the stale, pungent smell of smoke filled my nose. "Com'on in, Miz Valente, it's damn cold out there!" As was expected a cigarette, a permanent fixture, was jammed in the side of her mouth.

"Why Albert! I'll be! I ain't seen much of you lately. You

look chilled and peaked." She puffed and the smoke rose across her unseeing eye. "I guess you're still workin' on the ole homestead, ain'tcha?"

She scrutinized Albert. He nodded and quietly walked past her to a table in the corner of the store. He removed his brown wool fedora. Fannie seemed to feel the distance in her friend. It was then she must have realized I was there to join him.

"Well, ain't this nice," she said shutting the door. The metal bell at the top corner clanked. "Let me put another piece of wood in that stove." She lightly went on. "Poor ole thing gets a work-out this time of year."

Even with a slight limp, Fannie moved with a certain grace. At one point, she must have been an eye-catching woman. The years had claimed her physical health but not her vitality and gusto for life. It's funny how it is when you first meet a variety of people and think they're unattractive, but as you come to know them a sense of inner beauty far surpasses the outer peel. This was Fannie.

"Albert! I just made a fresh pot, I'm gonna pour you one. How about you, Miz Valente? Say, may I call you by your first name?"

I thanked her for the offer and told her my name.

She smiled softly. "Ain't that pretty. I like that. Carmela. Italian?"

I nodded.

"A lot of Italians worked in these here mines. Couple of nice families live up on the ridge." She wore the same clothing as the first day I met her, a stretched-out purple wool sweater and blouse over jeans. "You say that was your grandma's name? You liked her, didn'tcha?"

I replied yes and told her a little about my family.

"I had me a good granny. I remember she'd give me special

notice, even though she got so little appreciation herself." She shook her head. "It's a sorry mess how we allow girl-children to think they ain't as good as men. Don't know what that's all about. Sad thing is, it's the women that teach us. You know, the older I get, the more I understand what that thing they call the 'glass ceiling' is." She looked past me to where Albert sat. "Now Albert, you don't know what we're talkin' about, do ya?"

Albert answered quietly, still visibly shaken from the past hour's emotive upheaval. "I do know, Fannie. I do."

I leaned over the counter to draw Fannie closer out of Albert's earshot. I confided that he had just visited his family's gravesite and was rather upset and would need some smooth conversation to help him over a few rough spots. She hastily acknowledged my meaning.

Albert sat mesmerized. I wondered if our ability to chat and reach so rapidly into each other's lives perplexed him.

"Frank, Jr.," Fannie called suddenly into the squawk-box. "Carl Fenster is goin' to need his truck by noon. Ya think you'll be done?"

"Yeah, Ma," he answered from the garage. "I just need to change a couple of these spark plugs, and she'll be up and runnin' fine."

"Damn good kid. I'm gonna miss him. Loneliness is one bitter pill to swaller. How about you, Carmela? Ya ever bin lonely?"

I nodded. Fannie had asked the big question. Lonely. Even though my devoted husband had supported me, and many friends surrounded me, I was still starved. That undefined hunger had followed me for years, gnawing and setting its teeth into my soul. I looked at Albert. His open lonesomeness was pulling at the last shred of attachment he had to his wives and children.

*"Momma, talk to me."*

*Why do I feel so alone when I'm in the room with her? It's as if she doesn't even know I'm here. Why can't she just tell me she loves me?*

How old was I when I first understood that my mother would never love me? It didn't take too long.

Albert said, "It takes too much work to stay on top of being alone."

"Sure, it takes work," Fannie continued as she walked towards his table. "Everyday ya get up and you're faced with the same set of regulations, and unless ya wake up and adjust some of them rules, ain't nothin' gonna change. That's what its gonna take to shake this misery, Albert."

I flinched when she addressed him. I worried about his present vulnerability. But I felt he knew Fannie's motives. I followed Fannie to the table as she carried three mugs of the hot coffee. Her bent cigarette ash was ready to fall, but oddly it stayed.

Everything has its control factor. It's for all of us to find our control factors. I looked at these two people who'd so recently come into my life, and was suddenly struck with wonder at how fragile we humans are, how certain events can quickly change our stability. I listened as Fannie drew Albert into our conversation.

"I don't remember ever talking this openly or freely," Albert said. "How did you both get so wise and savvy?" The color was finally returning to his cyanic lips.

"Now if that means horse sense, you're right. I guess the kicks in the head help." Fannie grabbed a third chair. "I can't settle for numb. You gotta keep your head above the brown stuff. If you don't wise up, you'll never find that pig in all the slop."

Albert grinned. "You've always had a way of putting things, Fannie." He turned to me. "Ms. Valente," he began., "Sorry, I mean Carmela. Fannie is about as strong a gal as I know, other than Elsa Maas and Etta Mae at the motel. She has an understanding about things. I haven't been around this village for a long time, so I'm not really up on all that has happened in the years since I left, but I do know that she's had plenty of heartaches."

Fannie listened carefully. "You got that right, Albert, but no more than you. Don't skirt the subject, losing them babies and two wives ain't no small pickin's. Thing is, you got to look it all straight in the face, or you're as good as dead, yerself. I've been watchin' how you're actin', like it's all been sorted through, but I know different."

We all jumped when a gust of wind blew open the door, bringing in bone-chilling air. Fannie moved swiftly to close it.

"Where was I?" she said without missing a beat. "As a matter of fact, there's a few in this town is good at puttin' on a 'ain't no big thing' face. Crap happens, dammit! You can't ignore it." She stood up and paced the wooden floor. "I realize that we all been touched awfully bad in one way or another, especially here in Pine Grove Haven."

Fannie's emphysemic voice filled the room. Albert sat motionless, his face unreadable. I was unsure what influence her words would have. I nervously drank my coffee as Fannie delivered her sermon.

"Now you know, Albert, Amy was a good girl. Don't' forget that crazy family she came from. You needed to find out the truth. She needed protectin'. She was heart-broke after those babies died. Them damn talkin' mouths can slit a body with their sharp words."

Fannie struck tender cords. Albert smoothed his full head of hair with both hands. I cringed at the sight of the unhappiness returning to his red-rimmed eyes. I was worried about his inability to handle any more pressure today.

"It's not that you didn't love her; damn, we all knew that. But she was papery thin in her ways of thinking. You treated her like the children. Your pride and anger took over your thinkin'." Her hands fanned the air. "You wouldn't listen. Daisy Hinkle tried to tell you. You just made up your mind and that was that."

Fannie knew a great deal more about Amy than I realized.

"Daisy told me everythin'. She was the only one that Amy would let into the house after that unhappy day. She tried to help. But for some reason, Amy wanted to protect that sonna'-bitch. She wouldn't tell anyone who he was, not even Daisy. But I think Daisy guessed."

I remembered Daisy's written account. She was careful not to name a specific person. I heard blood rushing past my ears to that part of my brain that called for steadiness.

Albert looked up. His penetrating eyes seem to sear into Fannie's. His voice lost its calm. "What are you trying to tell me, Fannie? It was Farley, Amy's cousin, wasn't it? But, I don't have any proof. She wouldn't say. He was a scoundrel, though. He was always playing around, making trouble with young girls. Who was it?" he demanded.

My heart left its safe spot. I sensed the dreadful drama about to unfold. I reached for Albert's arm and tried to soothe him.

"Naw, it 'tweren't Farley. I can't say for sure, but it 'tweren't Farley. But I got a pretty good idea. I don't want to spread any untruths! But what I am sayin' is all that matters is that Amy weren't doin' nothin' wrong. You hear? Just mindin' those babies and this fool wouldn't stay away from her. He was tryin' to engage her in some antics, but she were fightin' him off."

Fannie stood up and moved about as she continued her rant.

"She tried to tell him that them babies were alone in the garden. But he wouldn't let her go! She were afraid to tell ya. Afraid you might just kill him, and people would hold her answerable. In the end, they blamed her anyway."

"Jeesus! Do you know what you're saying, Fannie? If you know, tell me! Why didn't I know this? Why didn't you tell me before now?"

Fannie came nearly nose-to-nose and waved her glowing fag at him, her other hand on her hip. "What makes you think you would have listened with both ears, Albert Schoen?"

I didn't need to speak. This was an exchange that was ancient. This was an exchange of veterans. This was the exchange of dialogue that was hard to face. This one, I knew.

"Why was she afraid of me? I wouldn't have hurt her."

"Hell, Albert, you had yours and her life all figured out! Amy was messin' up your plans by being down after those babies died. She needed you worse than ever. You were deaf as a doorknob. It was easier for you to listen to those cockroaches who didn't give a hoot—those honey-coated mouths, drippin' poison."

Fannie stopped. Her stance resolute. The silence blaring.

"I can't believe this," Albert hissed, his lips clenched tight across his teeth. "All these goddamn years. She could have told me."

"*Harrumph!* My fat foot!"

His stricken face recharged. "I'm going to find this bastard, Fannie! You know who he is don't you? You'd better tell me, or I'll hunt him out, by God! I'll hunt him out!"

"An' then what, Albert Schoen? An' then what? Should we just add to the carcasses?"

Venera Di Bella Barles

# *Excerpts from the Diaries of Miss Daisy Maude Hinkle*

**1956—October**

Dora and Carl are having problems with Merle. He keeps running away. He won't do his studies or help with the chores.

I asked him, when he was little, what he wanted to be when he grew up. He said, "I'm going to be a lion tamer." One never knows what will come out of children's mouths. I don't think he will stay still long enough to do much of anything.

•

**1956—November**

Nell Miller lost another of her babies. That makes five. Terrible for her—she looks so sad. Ma went to visit her today and brought her some honey bread. It doesn't seem right that some families have too many children and Nell can't seem to keep one.

Not too much fairness in this life.

•

**1957—August**

The suffocating temperature went sky high this week. Everything is extreme here in this valley.

Marlee Lou and I are going to help some of the younger women tomorrow with the clothing drive. We've been friends since we were young girls.

All kinds of people coming to work the mines and their families are in such desperate need. The more we battle for fairness, and the more we scrape the surface, the more we see further needs.

•

**1957—September**

It feels so very good to have another friend such as Fannie. She seems to be doing fine with Mr. Houston's old place. She's has the business back on its feet.

Fannie has been through so much in her young life. Four children before she was hardly in her twenties. She's gruff, but pure of heart. She said she used to put newspaper under the children's shirts to help them stay warm.

My, my, what is wrong with this country? People are willing to work hard but can't make enough to take care of themselves. I wonder if the Rockefellers ever think of us here in these hills of death. They talk about slavery in the south – but do they know about the slavery here in our coalmines?

# *Chapter 12*
# *The Visitation*

The smoke-yellowed motel room was dank and dismal. I stared at the rust and avocado green bedspread and wondered how many wandering souls had used this interim housing?

My head throbbed. I dampened a washcloth and placed its coolness on my forehead. Once more, I felt the seams of this community unraveling as more of the ugliness and darkness seeped through.

I could leave. I didn't need to be part of these imbroglios. I could walk away from these emotional poundings—the heck with these Hinkles, Schoens, and Maases. I had my own worries.

Except I knew my pattern, and it was not that simple. I could never walk away from broken wings.

Albert needed to open his eyes. Fannie was so right. She had exceptional wisdom and guts. How I could have used, in my earlier years, a straight-shooting caring person like her. How many times I could have used guidance with my thoughts. Those I thought would step forward to soothe me dropped the ball. Instead, the one individual I never expected to come forth gave me a go-ahead to grieve over the death of my son—so hard to understand why we need permission.

The next morning, I woke early, showered, dressed, and grabbed coffee and a bran muffin at the café. Locals sat with their morning brew, eyeballing me. Even ten-miles away, the word was out that I was nosing around Pine Grove Haven.

I needed to get back to that farm. Daisy Maude Hinkle wrote that story for a reason. Even as a young woman, Daisy shed light on masked issues. This rural community had all the facets of a large, complicated city.

As I drove, it was good to see the sun still hanging around and I could see for miles in the clearness of the day. The bleak landscape left many colors unused on the artist's palette. The snow had melted, exposing ruts on the hardpan dirt road. How many times had the Hinkle women traveled this road past the rusted mailbox that read ***S. HINKLE****?*

Selma, who acted as caretaker, gave me permission to visit as I required. This time I knew I needed to approach with a more critical eye. The question was constantly there; what was I looking for? What was the definitive statement that would wrap it into a fine, usable package? I wanted to clear up this nagging feeling that there was something I had to find. And an even more absurd notion that had taken hold of me, that only I could find *it* whatever *it* was. Only I, in some way I didn't understand, could set these women free.

They were just a hard working family in a labor-intensive community. I thought of Samuel Hinkle, who gave his *nth* to insure his family's welfare, a father, who was afraid he would lose control of them–who stole from his daughter Rose. A mother that knew her place, making sure her offspring understood their essential duties, but looked the other way when wrong was being done to them. A young son who never tasted life and Lily, a youthful daughter, who, having read the writing on the wall, decided to make her life outside this cocoon. And then there were the three other daughters, who, with their self-imposed spinsterhood, bypassed the gratification of the love of men and the pangs of childbirth.

As I went up the steps, I saw the door ajar—had I forgotten to close it the last time?

I stepped inside and called out.

It was colder indoors—like walking into a warehouse freezer. I scanned the rooms quickly. How strange that I felt I'd become the guardian of this home.

Something was wrong. Daisy's writings were strewn about the floor.

I inspected the stack. Someone was searching for something in these papers. Systematically, I plowed through and examined the clippings and narratives. Whoever it was, was in a hurry. Where was the small journal? I distinctly remembered setting it on the edge of the windowsill. I bent down to look under the table. Papers had fallen between it and the window ledge.

Could it be? Yes, the diary was missing. I blinked to clear my eyes. I had a feeling I was not alone, that someone was watching me. As if an invisible entity was scrutinizing my every move. I glanced down and saw a letter from Lily Hinkle, dated a few days before her sisters died. My heart thumped as if it were outside my chest. I realized it could be the last letter received.

Dear Violet, Rose, and Daisy,

I know I haven't seen you since spring, sorry but I can't make it back up there until after Christmas. My new bookshop is taking most of my efforts. I'm having such a good time and I'm selling a fabulous amount. People say I'm a natural for this business. I'll mail you the newspaper clipping with my picture.

Love,
Lily

I walked into the kitchen to the area where the sisters were found, next to the massive black and chrome wood burning stove. I pulled my jacket closer about me. I could still feel an unnerving presence. Even the air was unexpectedly chillier. The lump in my throat had swollen. I was afraid to look. I sensed it was Daisy. I turned around quickly. Whatever or whoever had stood behind me was gone.

*Is that you, Daisy? What's going on?*

How perfectly silly, I thought. What are you afraid of, Carmela? Now you're seeing things that aren't there. You don't believe in ghosts.

Maybe Selma had come to check on what I'd been prying into.

I peered out the window. There was no one.

My imagination certainly was working overtime, but the

journal was gone. Someone had been looking for information.

I left the kitchen and sat on a tapestry rocker in the small, drab parlor to chew on some thoughts. Someone else was interested in these notes and papers. It could be Albert. He was so angry. Daisy didn't say who the bounder was in the Schoen house that catastrophic day. But Fannie seemed to think she knew. Why didn't she say? Even she seemed to be shielding the person. I found it interesting that Albert thought it was Amy's cousin.

Dingy, crocheted antimacassars laced the back of two overstuffed chairs. There was talent and aptitude in this house. Besides the many handmade creations stashed in different parts of the home, these women were writers, outspoken heralds who protected miners against wrongs. Dedicated seekers of truth. It would stand to reason that they would care what happened to their neighbors and Amy.

When I left the living room, I turned again to look through the stack of papers and writings. Daisy was clever. Her disguised notes were making more sense, or else I was reading too many crime stories. With intent she had changed the names and some facts in her stories to disguise the true incidents.

Now, I was sure why I was here.

I moved a pile of papers aside to make space, when suddenly I saw the penknife. I knew it had not been there before. I saw the initials engraved in the bone handle. My legs weakened. My suspicions were confirmed.

I slipped the well-patined knife into my jeans pocket, the initials tickled my fingertips. Now, I was the keeper of secrets and suspicions—memories came back with a poignancy of long ago, memories of my own clandestine family sagas. I knew I could never talk to anyone of the clouded paths of some of my relatives. I was schooled very young never to air our family's transgressions. No one had to tell me—but I knew. It was understood that we keep a smooth, and fake, exterior.

Once more, I looked at Lily's communication. What business was it of mine to stir the natives? Who appointed me judge and jury?

"You're one busy gal, now ain'tcha, Miz Valente?"

I dropped the letter and nearly flew out of my boots. It was Carl Fenster. A foot behind me, looming tall with his arms crossed. I wondered how long he had been standing there. Beside him stood his Labrador, Satin.

"Now wouldn't it be better to just let these poor folks settle in their graves instead of you churning up their dust?"

He glowered at me. I told him I was sorry but I wasn't the only one searching for information.

"What you mean?" He moved closer to see what I was reading. "You say someone else's diggin'?" Carl interrupted my answers. "What in the hell for?"

I told him I wasn't sure who or why. I didn't want to tell him about the knife. I guardedly asked him how he thought the community would handle the truth about a certain situation.

"What? What kind of sit'ation? What the hell are you talkin' about? And what makes you think you a better thinker than the rest of us folks? Sometimes it's best to leave them sleepin' dogs just lie. No sense in rakin' stuff that don't help nobody. Seems you're a little nosy. I thought you came for information about them Hinkle girls."

Carl Fenster was frightening me. He had turned stern and mean. I wondered if his defensiveness wasn't part of a cover-up. I again made my apologies to Carl and conveyed to him that he was probably right about rattling cages. Anyway I was just about through with my note gathering. I told him I would most likely be leaving in a few days.

"Not a bad idear! I ain't seen this town this upset for a long time. I think all this diggin' around is unhealthy."

I felt scolded. The embarrassment compounded my misery. Satin strolled by my side and licked my hand.

"I hear a new humdinger of a storm is headin' this way. Don't want to get stuck now, do ya?"

The door slammed. I jumped and quickly turned. Satin gave three barks.

"You're kind of spooked, now ain'tcha? That was just the wind. You're actin' like you're expectin' somebody."

I admitted I was indeed more wary than usual, and that it was hard to be in this Hinkle house with all of its memories. But I did feel that I knew the sisters better. I told him how drawn I was to understand the Schoen tragedy as well. I gently asked him if he wouldn't want to find the underlying reason for the Hinkle deaths, or the unidentified wrongdoer in the Schoen tragedy.

His stance relaxed. "*Hmmm.* I guess these god-awful deaths have buffaloed this valley. I mean, not that we haven't had a mess of dyin' around here, but when you know somethin' ain't right with a report, it gnaws at your brain. I think the ole girls was just tired of living. That's what I think. They weren't getting around much any more and for sure sister Lily just about abandoned them. They was lonely. I see that. I told you about my Dora, didn't I?"

He looked beyond me to the kitchen floor and drew in deeply on his pipe, the smoke floated above my head. He missed his wife. I missed my husband.

I stopped listening. The smell of his sweet tobacco made

my thoughts drift. I considered how appealing and needy it was for people to covet their smokes, like suckling at a mother's breast.

"Satin, you come here, girl. I don't want you in that kitchen, you hear?" He bent to pet her, and then straightened up again. "The truth is, I ain't slept well since these women died, nar over a year now. It was bad enough losing my Dora."

Gloom crossed his face. His shoulders suddenly slumped. I asked him what he thought was the problem.

"I wished I knew!"

He took the smoking pipe in and out of his mouth and then fell silent for a long moment.

His voice quavered as he continued, "Were we good friends? Yeah, we was. I hated to tell them that I couldn't afford to raise grain on their land any longer. Maybe, they'd still be alive. They was countin' on that money. They seemed so shot down. I think they was feeling like they was helpin' me by leasin' that property. Maybe they felt like there was no reason to hang around anymore. Like nobody needed them."

Carl walked to the kitchen and stared at the stove. "Dammit! What a goddamn curse!"

I approached him, but I was nervous. I told him how quick we are to take on guilt for someone else's actions. I asked him if he purposely set out to hurt Violet, Rose, and Daisy.

"Me? Hell, no! I'd sooner shoot myself."

Then, I asked, didn't he think the women had some responsibility in their own deaths?

"Well, I suppose. But I should of protected them. I just didn't see it comin'. It smacked me so hard, I felt like a killer. It was too much. Lord, I didn't want it to end that way. When I saw those three girls on that floor, I nearly died myself."

He trembled as he moved away from the room towards

Daisy's writing alcove. Satin sensing that his paternal friend was sad, nudged his hand and leg.

"Who would of thought they'd do anythin' like that? They didn't pay their electric bill, so they couldn't turn on the electric heater. No reason for that type of stupid thinkin'. Selma and some of the other ladies always checked on them, and they'd just send them away.

He collapsed in a straight-back wicker chair by the frosted window, and with his chapped hand tapped his tobacco-filled pipe on the ledge. I acknowledged the anguish of it all. I told him how dreadful my father had felt because he insisted his young, sick cousin attend a gathering. She died soon afterwards, and the guilt of her death followed him forever.

There was a dramatic stillness in the house as we both sat without further words, mulling our heart tales. Satin seemed to understand the melancholy in the room.

"Gettin' awful cold out there. Awful cold. Are ya findin' anythin'?"

His voice toned down and he bent to pick up some of the fallen papers.

"How did this stuff get thrown around?"

I explained that this was the way I found the papers this morning. It appeared someone else had an interest in finding something.

"What? Are ya sayin' that whoever was in here, besides you, messed this place like this?"

I nodded.

"Well, I'll be dammed. *Huh*. Maybe someone *is* worried."

The light faded, and I told Carl I had to leave soon. I wasn't sure if he heard me. I picked up my purse and flipped my wool scarf around my neck.

"I guess you're callin' it a day, heh, Miz Valente? By the

way, thanks for the kind words. What say? Headin' for Fannie's place? Right. Right. She's a good ole girl. Just a little too colorful to suit my tastes. I hear you're havin' supper later with Selma Webster and her daughter."

As usual news was on the move.

He bent and petted Satin. "Com'on ole girl, we got chores to do and supper to cook." I was glad Carl left me to myself.

As the echoes of Carl's footsteps faded, I walked into the kitchen to the area again. The sun hid behind a cloud and dimmed the room. A sudden cold wave of air drifted across my face and body. My mind imagined the sisters' conversation as they carried out their duties on their final day:

*"Violet. Violet, do you think Amy will bring her little ones over for a visit? We must get Carl to plow the road or Father will be angry".*

*"Rose, now don't you worry your head about that. Daisy and I are taking care of things."*

*"Where is Lily?"*

*"Just received a letter from Pittsburgh. Sister Lily says she won't be able to get here until after Christmas. She's just can't get away from her new store. She says she's selling quite a few of the used books."*

*"Hmmm. Now, isn't that nice, Violet? Daisy, you're the one who should have a book shop. Someday they'll publish your stories, isn't that right, Daisy?"*

*"Yes, Rose, I suppose someday they will. Now bring that shawl closer around your neck, dear. Your fingers are like cold sticks."*

*"We'll have to take the vegetables to market soon, won't we? Do you think father will be home soon? Sometimes I'm afraid of him, Daisy."*

*"I know, dear. Don't worry, Rose, we're here to protect you."*

*"Violet, we have just a few more pieces of wood left. I don't know*

*if we can hold up to this coldness."*

*"Daisy, I think we should finish the logs tonight. Do you think you'll be ready?"*

*"Yes, Violet, I think I am. I think I am..."*

They were holding Rose's hands...they were protecting her.

Venera Di Bella Barles

# *Excerpts from the Diaries of Miss Daisy Maude Hinkle*

**1958—February**

I am numb once again with yet another report.

An explosion killed sixteen miners. They sent in a rescue party of some forty men who entered the mine, but a second explosion slashed through and trapped the rescuers. Only two were saved. The mine had to be sealed with the bodies inside.

Does anyone care, outside of these hills, how it feels to seal live bodies into a tomb? Sometimes I wake at night and hear their cries beneath my feet.

•

**1958—March**

Thomas was written up in the weekly mining paper. He's a hero for saving four trapped miners. He truly is a gentle and valiant man.

Thomas says they have some mine rats as big as powder kegs. He said the miners feel safe as long as the rats are running over their feet and hanging around their dinner pail. The rats sense any changes and settling of the roof that comes before a cave-in, so when they scurry, the men follow. But the rats are also a terrible nuisance. He says conditions are so much better than they were when he was a boy.

•

**1958—April**

Violet and I visited Amy's and the twins' graves today. It's been five years this day since she died, one year after her babies—almost to the hour. She was so mal-nourished and couldn't ward off the pneumonia that killed her.

It's been a few years since Albert left for New York. Guess it's too blame hard to come back here from New York. He sends me cards and letters, always asks how everyone is. Maybe it was easier to leave all this hurting. He came the first year to visit their graves, but, after that, less and less. We hear he is doing very well for himself.

I'm glad someone can make his or her way out of this cut of hell.

# Chapter 13
# His Brother's Keeper

Fannie's store was busy. Folks hastened to pick up last minute emergency supplies of batteries, kerosene, and emergency flares. The air was crisp and laden with the impending snow change. Aching minds and shoulders felt it. In winter, the weather made most of the decisions in this unsympathetic land. The one good thing about snow was that it covered the worn-out structures and grayness of the town.

I could see a "Gottschalt's Gas and Variety Store" sign painted on the side of the building under an old Sonoco logo. I pulled to a stop, and then sat in my car for a time studying the scene and customers. The blinking "open" neon sign was already turned on. A large, oil tanker had filled the holding tanks with gas and was just pulling out. A middle-aged couple that I last saw at the church gathering stood at the counter with their purchases. I recognized a few other patrons in the store, and then I noticed Albert's brother, John Schoen. With his sharp-features and handsome face, he looked like a well-worn copy of his brother, Albert. Even though I'd spent an evening with him and his family, I hadn't talked in depth with him. He seemed to take a step back around his brother.

How did he assess their lives? What were his opinions concerning the family tragedies?

"Say, are you comin' in, or are you trying to freeze your eyeballs?"

Fannie's voice startled me as she rapped on the car window. I hadn't seen her come out the door. I told her I didn't want to bother her, knowing she was busy with customers. I just wanted to chat a bit if she had time.

"Oh, for gosh sakes! You ain't takin' any skin off nobody's nose. Just get in here. I got the stove cranked up. John Schoen is back in there."

I came through the door, acknowledged the couple leaving, and nodded to another lady with her little girl. Minnie, the tabby, greeted me with a leg rub. I bent to pet her, glad for the warm recognition. I greeted John Schoen, and then I sat down in a chair nearby. Minnie immediately jumped into my lap.

He meekly smiled and without looking at me said, "I like to write, too. Didn't have much of an education to do much with. Ain't had the schoolin' Albert had." John played with the zipper of his jacket as he talked. "What have you written?" He asked.

He sat near me as I warmed my hands on the cup of black coffee. He was more relaxed now than on the day that I'd come to his home for dinner. I gave him an account of my background in journalism and my desire to write another novel. I had written many short stories and added a small stipend to my retirement with freelance articles in various magazines and journals. He listened carefully. In turn I asked him how he got started writing.

He bowed his head and fidgeted with the leather gloves he'd picked off the table. Out of nowhere he began to share, what I believed, were well-sealed opinions and ideas.

"Well, I saw a lot happening, so I began keeping notes about the folks in this county. Seems like there is enough stories to pick from and it takes a lot of time to do what you like, doesn't it?"

I nodded and removed my scarf and hat. I told him if you love something, you must make time for it.

"You say that right. My father made us learn, even though we worked the mines," he said. "Albert and I had to help him. Pretty hard work. When we were done with our schoolwork we could read books. We borrowed them from the Hinkle sisters. Now, I like to read whenever I can. Of course, Albert has a better education."

John turned to me, holding my gaze a little longer than I was used to. It was as if he were checking to see how I reacted to his statement about Albert. The moment felt peculiar. It was uncommon for many of these people to maintain eye contact. I inquired again about his writing.

"Well, it was Daisy Hinkle that pushed me to put words to paper. I like to write about the mine and its workers. So did she. Awful lot happened down in those god-forsaken holes. It's another world."

I nodded. I imagined there were many stories. He seemed pleased and more relaxed to be talking to me about himself.

"I keep a notebook right here in my shirt pocket and write down a note or two when something comes to mind. What are you gonna write about us here in Pine Grove Haven? I hope its not distorted facts."

The sharp jibe surprised me. I asked what that meant. Did he believe I was here to skew the truth?

"Well, you know it's not easy to find where the truth is in all the garbage that people make. God knows the truth is needed here. But no one has the backbone to state it."

I asked him why.

"Miss Valente, I wish I could say. I wish I could say. I don't interfere in things not my affair. I'm only sayin' that I wish things were different. Albert has been fairly upset this week. I'd say since you been here. That's what I would say. Maybe, it's best sometimes to leave folks alone. Ha, I guess you can tell I'm not much of a man if I tell you that. Too much stirrin' of memories. I don't know what to think." The scar on his right temple turned a deep scarlet.

Fannie overheard John. Most of the customers were now gone.

She moved close to him. She coughed loudly to clear her throat. "No use to blame this here gal for the crap that was here before she came. Carmela's not responsible for the head buryin' goin' on in this town. Even you turned your head away from helpin' your brother. Remember? Can't nobody do what's right? Everybody's so almighty self-righteous on church goin' day, but the rest of the week is paved like the road to hell."

Fannie's cigarette flared between her fingers as she gestured wildly. The cat jumped off my lap, figuring it was time to find a safer place to park. "Even those damn ole women closed up in that beat-up house down in the holler'—folks knew they needed attention. They was gettin' decrepit and foolish. *Harrumph.* My fat foot they was helpin'. Makin' believe they was helpin' them. Somebody shoulda moved them out of that hellhole. Same as with me when I come here. They knew I needed help. I was alone with no work or money to save my children from starvation. I guess they thought I wasn't good enough to lend a hand to."

Her voice climbed a few decibels as her jowly cheeks and neck flushed.

John squirmed as Fannie spoke. He stood and removed his heavy fleece-lined coat and then shuffled about the coal dust encrusted floor. His eyes gleamed and blinked as he looked up to the ceiling at the now motionless, summer fan. "Now, Fannie, just you wait a minute – you don't know it all. If you knew so much, what did you do to make it right? We all took turns checking up on the Hinkles. For whatever reason, they decided enough was enough."

I flinched and moved my chair back from the table.

"And as for my sister-in-law and those children, Lord knows we all cried buckets – wasn't much we could do. Just a pitiful handout of misery."

"You could have stopped the crap pourin' out of people's mouths. Too busy protectin' the wrong folks and you know very well what I'm gettin' at."

"Fannie, Albert didn't want to know anything," John answered. "He was stubborn and set in his ways. Don't forget he was mourning the loss of his children, too. Everything was fuzzy about what happened that day with Amy."

"Clean your ears! Don't you hear? Nothing happened – she was just the target of vicious crap! Nobody wanted to know who the sonna-bitch was that was botherin' the hell out of her. They just jumped their minds to she did somethin' wrong. Well, I hope they all have eternal indigestion, now!"

Frank, Jr. came in from the garage wide-eyed. He could hear his mother's gushing temper. He headed for the coffee machine to pour a cup.

"Ma, let it go for Chrissake. You can't change what happened. Ain't nothing gonna change what happened. You tried to tell people, but they just ignored you."

"Frank, Jr., this ain't your affair."

John tried to redirect the conversation, "Fannie, calm down now. It's over. No use getting yerself riled up over past things."

"John, get your head out of your ass! It's still goin' on!"

**Venera Di Bella Barles**

# *Excerpts from the Diaries of Miss Daisy Maude Hinkle*

**1959—January**

What a way to start the New Year. An unbelievable accident happened in the Wilkes-Barre/Scranton area—the Knox Mine flood. We are all stunned. I've added this to my other news clippings—I'm certainly getting a collection. This was the write-up in the newspaper.

"The Susquehanna River broke through and flooded the underground anthracite mines after an operator dug under the river. A rich vein of anthracite lay under the riverbed at the village of Port Griffith, near Pittston. As miners worked upon this vein, the river smashed through and flooded the mine. Twelve miners were killed immediately, their bodies washed away in the flood, never to be seen again. There were seventy-four workers in the mine at the time of the calamity; sixty-two of them were able to escape by various means, some involving the highest heroism on the part of their co-workers. They had to relocate the Lehigh Valley Railroad. Moved more than thirty railcars and four-hundred mine cars in to plug the hole made by the break-through."

Just when you think it will get better...

# *Chapter 14*
# *Oh Death, Oh Death*

The quiet, well-behaved community, tucked into the coal-mining hills, was far from the settlement I now encountered. Its civilization was coming out from under their blanket of propriety. The framework the rural community so carefully constructed was shattering with each of my personal encounters. It was as if the villagers were waiting to find the escape vent to release years of pent-up secrets.

I felt the responsibility to weigh carefully how much of the sensitive details I should be allowed to hear. They didn't give the impression of holding back these last few days.

The car heater took a bit of time to reach even a minimal level of warmth. With each breath my nostrils felt the cutting cold. How difficult it must have been for these miners to work in the harshness and dampness of these hills.

It was twilight, when the world is outlined against the sky

and leafless stands of trees appear as giant warriors guarding the homes. I drove a quarter of a mile past the winding road that led down to the Hinkle patch, towards Selma Webster's small saltbox house. Billowing smoke poured from the leaning chimney. I was glad I had remembered to wrap the gifts.

Selma's rusted, green Buick was parked in the driveway. I walked up to the small cement stoop, and was about to knock on the door, when I heard what seemed to be a recording of a sorrowful a cappella wail of a bluegrass singer. I paused to listen to the singer ask death to spare him.

I waited a few more minutes. Then another medley, not quite as mournful, played with sounds of mandolins, guitars, and violins, singing about a dark, troubled life.

Memories floated back of my father singing the sad ballads of Sicily, called *Stornelli*. His songs spoke of his experiences of hard work in marble quarries, mines of a different sort. He sang of the misfortunes surrounding his people.

What would I encounter this evening with the Webster family?

"Well, now hi, Miz Valente. Thought I heard your car, but I didn't hear you knock. Come on in. I've got supper near ready. Marla, my girl, should be home from work soon."

I entered the spotless, run-down house and stood in the foyer, glancing about as I removed my heavy jacket. Benson, their elderly mixed poodle/terrier wagged his tail and needed his head rubbed. Selma had told me about their old dog that couldn't see or hear. Amazingly, he sure knew his way around. Too bad humans can't adjust as well. The aroma of baking biscuits and faint smell of onions wafted into my nose. The sort of smells from my childhood. As in most homes in the valley, there were family photographs on walls to validate lives. One could see the level of importance by the positioning and placement of the pictures.

I thanked Selma for inviting me.

"No need for thanks – everybody's gotta eat."

I handed her the packaged tea towels and three booklets of paper doll cutouts for the children.

"Well, what's this?" she asked, her eyes sparkling as I handed her the gifts. She held them tightly. "How nice. How nice."

As we walked past the parlor, she pointed where her three young grandchildren played on the floor with a board game. Benson had joined them. "This way, Miz Valente. Them's Marla's babies."

I followed her into the kitchen. She directed me to a chair. "Won't you sit?"

The table, dressed with a faded red-checkered cloth and set with chipped Blue Willow dishes, dominated the room. A vase of artificial daffodils sat in the center. Although everything was old and well-worn, all seemed carefully placed.

"Let me turn down this here music. My son, Phinney, gave me this here cassette player and tapes of bluegrass. I'm afeared I'm wearin' them out. I grew up with this, but I don't hear anyone sing much of it anymore. I've got kin in Tennessee and they real good at puttin' out foot stompin' tunes. My pappy used to play the fiddle and sing. Ma would sing backup. They could dance and shuffle up a storm. My sister, Sabina, writes the words for this fella, Gordy Lewis. He's put out a couple of records, played at the Opry. You like Bluegrass?"

I told her I did most certainly. I related how I grew up with my father's country melodies. I asked her not to turn off the music.

"*Huh*. I-talian. Don't believe I've ever heard any of that. Ain't it strange we all think our world starts at the 'welcome sign' to our town and ends as folks leave to get on the highway. Self-centered of us, ain't it?" she chuckled.

I asked her about her grandchildren and stated how hard it must be to have to raise small children again.

"Yep. People never know when they're gonna be called on to take the reins. Poor thins' was so close to their pa. Ain't nowhere safe. When the time comes you better have your hat ready. He was picked off in the prime of his life. On the way to Wilkes-Barre late one night, he fell asleep and drove that dang truck right into a tree. Poor Marla, she was stunned. She couldn't keep up the mortgage on the house. They foreclosed on it a couple of months ago. One false move and everybody's direction is changed. Ain't that right, Carmela? You sure that's all right to call you that?"

I reassured her, and she left the room to check the children. I could hear her comforting them.

"Supper's almost ready and your ma is comin' now don't you worry. Let's have a little squeeze, and I want you to come in here and meet Miz Valente. She brung you these nice cutouts. Now, you know what to do."

Three towheaded girls, holding hands, came into the kitchen and stared at me with questioning eyes. They were silent. Each had a large red taffeta bow anchored to her hair. Seeing these three girls struck me as a coincidental twist of fate to the three Hinkle sisters, holding hands.

"This is Katy, the oldest. She's six. And this is Maddy, four. And this here is Lizzy. She's three. Kin you say hello to Miz Valente? Now, com'on, don't be shy. She's a good lady."

They moved carefully towards me, grasping each other's hands and still did not speak, but stood dutifully in front of me, the dog by their side.

I could feel their fear. What a wretched thing it was to lose a father.

"I hear Marla comin'," Selma said. "Girls, your ma is here! You'll have to show her the new paper-doll books Miz Valente gave you."

It was as if someone had turned a magical key in the children's backs. Life poured into them when their mother, pink with the icy cold, walked through the front door.

Selma's daughter was lovely and sylph-like, though plainly dressed. Her almost white-blonde shoulder length hair was pulled back into a ponytail, away from her delicately sculpted features. She was close to thirty years old, but looked barely out of her teens. Marla bent as her children encircled her knees. Wordlessly, the four held each other close.

"Marla, this here is Miz Carmela Valente." Selma turned to me. "I been tellin' my daughter all about you, Carmela."

"Hiya!" she said without raising her head. "Pleased to meetcha. I knew you were stayin' over at the motel where I work. Sorry I'm late, Ma. I'll help you in a minute."

"No need. Things are ready. I just need to put the slaw on the table. Carmela, I have some of my canned peaches I want you to try. I'm gonna give a couple of jars to take home with you."

There was gentleness between the two women. I envied their obvious closeness. But it was sad to see how young Marla was to be left a widow with three little girls. What kind of a rotten card game is this—too many jokers in this deck of life.

I had been told the parlors were mostly for funerals, Sunday visits and other serious matters, as it was in my grandparents' home. I looked about. The kitchens in these homes were the hubs.

"I can't recall if you told me if your ma was still alive." Selma asked me. "My memory is slippin'. Hope you like pot roast, string beans, boiled potatoes, and carrots. Got an apple pie to go with it and plenty of coffee."

I told Selma my mother was gone and that, sadly, we never had a good relationship.

"I can't even picture not being close to your ma." She turned, looked directly into my eyes. "Didn't she like you? Some women are funny that way. A' feared of their daughters…like they is gonna take somethin' away from them. You know, green-eyed. Funny stuff, ain't it?

I didn't answer. I looked down. She had hit the target.

Marla came into the kitchen; her girls stood by her side. The littlest held her leg as Marla went about her duties. She never shooed them away. She knew they needed her body and scent. Or was it she required theirs?

At first, she was shy to start a conversation with me. I complimented her children on their prettiness and manners.

"They've a lot to learn," Marla responded. "You girls thanked Miz Valente for yer presents? Com'on now."

In unison the three girls responded, "Thank you, Miz Valente, for our paper dolls."

"Poor ma has got her hands full helpin' to take care of 'em. I don't know what I'd do without her."

I acknowledged the weightiness of her situation. I asked if she liked the work at the motel.

"I don't mind, but it don't pay enough to even buy a fly swatter. I'm gonna get me to school to see if I kin get a better job. Then, I'll be able to take care of us properly. I guess you know their pa is dead."

I nodded and expressed my condolences. I told her it must have been a terrible shock for her to lose her husband so young.

"This town knows widows real well," she said with a slight

choke in her voice. "Somehow I knew it wouldn't last. He was too good. He was like Pa."

Selma turned around holding a fork. "I'm tryin' to tell her not to give up hope. She'll love agin."

"Ma, who is gonna want some worn-out gal with three little girls to raise? Don't you see we can't keep men in this house or in this town?"

"*Huh*. Ain't that so."

They moved in a harmonious style about the kitchen. Each knew what was needed without directions. I could never work with my mother in our home without feeling in the way. Mother's criticisms were cutting.

"Albert Schoen's comin' over to the house later for pie and coffee. I told him you were comin' for supper, Carmela. He usually comes each week to look in on us. Good sort." She wiped her hands on her clean, but threadbare half-apron.

I wondered if his thoughts of revenge and adjustments had subsided.

"He kinda favors Marla, but she don't want to give an ear to that."

"Ma, now don't go sayin' things like that. He don't wanna bother with someone like me. He's too educated and besides he's an ole man."

"Ole man?" Selma looked hard-eyed at her daughter, over her wide plastic spectacles. "Your pa was twenty years better than me and we sure had a good life. He were good to you kids and me. I was fifteen when we married."

I felt Marla's embarrassment. The ageless attempt at matchmaking was active and kicking.

I asked Selma if I could help. "Well, you kin drain the potatoes and put them in this here bowl. Slap a little butter on the top. Do you like to cook?"

I appreciated her caring gentleness. I explained to her it used to be one of my favorite ways of taking care of my family. Living alone didn't spark any creativity, but I thought I was a good cook. I told her about how, in the days after my marriage, I had wanted to try all the different foods that hadn't been prepared in my family's home. What a treat to open cookbooks and experiment beyond my native dishes. It was difficult for me to tell what was appreciated when I had a family. They just ate and ran off. I never knew what they thought, except when they didn't like it.

"*Huh!* That's too bad but it do sound familiar for some folks. The world is sure filled with critics; not too many show up with roses. Ha. Well let's sit and start our *widders'* meal. Seems like we go to more funerals then weddins'."

We sat down. Selma sliced the pot roast, and passed it around. Marla fixed the children's plates. They waited quietly with their hands in their laps, always watching their mother for head nods and eye directions. If I asked them a question they would first look to their mother and then they would answer faintly. It's fascinating to note how some children understand the alpha part of their family without much stress, yet others wear their families down with their daunting, unearned authority. There was little doubt with my father, I always knew my rank.

Conversation moved freely. We talked about Marla's husband and how things were when she grew up with her brothers.

"Pa was a good man. Never an unkind word to Ma or us. Just worked and worked and worked. He wanted us to get educated, especially the boys. He was afraid they'd end up in the mines like him. My husband, Jake, was a good father and husband, too. Came from the next holler. We were doing pretty good. We bought us a house and it looked like a good life ahead of us. But it all changed in one day."

We all fell quiet.

"It's hard for some folks to even realize when they're loved," Selma remarked. "It was never a mystery in our family, isn't that right, Marla?" She looked at her daughter with admiration and satisfaction. "We always hugged and let each other know just how we felt. Took the guessin' out of the game."

"Ma and Pa was our backbone," Marla said. "We didn't have to wonder which direction we were goin'. And there was no doubt Jake loved me and the girls."

Marla put down her cutlery and stared at me. She was wholesome and naturally beautiful. She seemed to want more from me. Her wide eyes expressed more than words. If she were in Los Angeles, or in New York City, advertising jockeys would have snatched a face and body, like hers.

"Ma says you're writin' a book about us here in Pine Grove Haven. Why us? Do you think we're strange?"

Selma looked up. "Now Marla, Carmela is tryin' to understand who we are. Ain't that right? She's tryin' to find out why them Hinkle girls did that thing a year ago. I'm sure they got the same type of characters in any town—just with other names." She sat straight in her chair and passed more coleslaw. Her daughter held the dish, while I scooped a spoonful. The grandchildren listened while they ate. Benson roamed around under the table.

Selma's wisdom continued. "The world is a lot smaller than we think. People have problems just like us, and anyone who thinks they're superior just has bigger closets to hide their lies. Ain't that right, Carmela?"

I smiled and agreed. Selma, like Fannie, Etta Mae and Elsa,

was no slouch in the "truth and tell it like it is department." We spoke for quite some time about their collective friends and how choices had affected all their lives.

"Lord knows we have made some rotten decisions, but some people have a real knack for it. Do you wish you had done things different, Carmela?" Selma asked after we'd finished our meal.

I nodded. They watched me carefully as I removed my cardigan sweater and adjusted my jewelry.

"Too hot? These stoves throw off a lot of heat," Selma remarked.

Marla looked intently at my neck. "Your necklace and earrings are pretty, Carmela. I wished I was smart enough to write or do somethin' with my life."

I thanked her for the compliment, admonished her for her lack of confidence. I back-tracked to Marla's previous question of "why us." I told her that at first I was under the mistaken belief that Pine Grove Haven was unusual, but everyday I peeled back another layer of their personalities, I was fascinated by the similarities of our lives.

"Well, I guess you're right," Marla said. "We just have our ways of handlin' stuff."

I heard the sound of tires mashing the snow. Katy, Maddy, and Lizzy looked up in anticipation. Suddenly their eyes glistened.

"Ma!" Maddy called. "It's Mr. Schoen. He's come agin'. Kin we show him our paper dolls?"

"Now, you girls hush and mind your manners. You can show 'em after awhile. Just let him settle in."

"Kin we get up, Ma?" asked Katy.

The room filled with the eagerness of Albert's arrival. Selma rose to answer the knock as her granddaughters tagged behind. Marla fixed some loose strands of her hair and then without speaking cleared the dinner plates

I could hear the commotion in the front entry. The girls squealed with guileless cheer. I listened to Albert's soft, engaging voice responding.

"Mr. Schoen, Miz Valente is here and she brung us paper dolls! Ain't they purdy?"

"Lovely, Katy."

"Kin you read us a story agin tonight?" Lizzy asked.

"I don't know if I will tonight, but I promise I will be back to read you two stories another evening. How's that?"

They walked in step beside Albert into the kitchen as if they were protecting him.

"Well, Carmela, we meet again. You're looking lovely, as usual." He turned to Marla, standing quietly at the sink. "How are you doing, Marla. Had a hard day?"

With a blush she answered, "Not too bad, Mr. Schoen."

"Albert," he smiled. "No need for Mr. Schoen, Marla." He turned to me. "I knew Marla when she was just a child, but she still insists on formalities."

As was typical of Albert, he was well-groomed, with the scent of toilet water. I looked at Marla as he spoke. She was uneasy as she fluttered about the room keeping busy. But I could see there was a sparkle in her eyes.

"Sit down, Albert. Coffee? Kin I fix you plate of pot roast, got plenty."

"No, thanks, Selma. *Mmmm,* smells like you all had a good supper. I'll just have coffee. So what have you fine folks been gossiping about?"

"Gossipin'? Why tain't what we did at all. Just tellin' Carmela here about our family and common known facts about our town."

I remembered the last time I saw Albert, that explosive meeting at Fannie's. I had thought he would never calm down.

The three children sat propped on his lap. The faint sound of bluegrass played in the background, set on repeat cycle. "Girls, Mr. Schoen don't need you all over him like that," Marla said. "Com'on, get off." She reached to take Lizzy, the youngest, off his knee. But his hand grabbed her arm gently.

"Please, Marla, let them stay," he pleaded.

I watched once more how losses were soothed. Lizzy laid the side of her face on his chest. Albert patted her head.

Selma broke in, "Howya been doin' down at your house, Albert? Last time I looked, you was replacin' some windows and addin' a stoop in the back."

"I've finished. Just need to paint, come spring. But, lately, I'm not sure I want to stay in that house. Too many memories. I may rent it out again and build elsewhere. I'm still trying to decide."

"You've not been happy here, have you? You seem awfully unsettled in the last couple of days."

"I expect I am, but we've all been through a lot, haven't we, Selma? Time for me to open my eyes wider, I suppose."

"There's truth there."

I apologized for the possibility that all my digging about might have caused an intrusion into their lives. I wanted them to know how deeply I cared for them.

"You mustn't blame yourself, Carmela, for what needed to be looked at," Albert replied. "You were merely the catalyst. I buried my feelings along with the family."

Marla looked at me then sipped her coffee slowly. "How is your family, Carmela? Do you like living alone and doing for yerself? I'm sure there is plenty of heartache to go around."

I quickly answered yes. I wanted to tell them more. Suddenly my mind shot in all directions. Questions began to fill my head. I could hear them talking but I was much too involved with my own thoughts. Was I happy? Was I always running because I was lonely?

I loved my life, but there was something missing—was it someone to share it with more intimately? I missed family. I reminded myself that I needed to get closer to my daughters and grandchildren. I looked at Albert and realized I had passed up many opportunities for a man's companionship, not necessarily to marry. A male puts a different slant on feelings and life.

Albert, Selma, and Marla seemed at ease with their conversation. Albert was much calmer than I had seen him at Fannie's. The children pulled their chairs close to him and Katy, the oldest, began to cut out paper dolls for her sisters. Lizzy continued to sit on his lap. I asked him about the house he was repairing.

"I had it rented out for a few years. It needed a lot of work, but it's looking much better, now. I remodeled the kitchen and put in a sun porch." He clasped his hands around his coffee cup and looked over at the children. "Amy loved the house."

"Maybe, it is too blame hard being there with all them recollections," Selma remarked. "I mean after being away so long and then to come back to all those ole ghosts. I don't know that I could last long in a place like that. What was you thinkin'?"

"Well, it *is* a fine home, I just need to get settled a little more. I really do like this area. I've had enough of big city living, and I wanted to come to peace and quiet. I think I'll be better soon. Besides, Fannie has given me hell about my thinking. So, I had best wake up to facts. Isn't that right, Carmela? I couldn't sleep a wink last two nights trying to sort out all these crazy thoughts."

I smiled and told him there was much to plow through; careful to avoid any words that would bring him back to anger.

Selma squinted at Albert. "Fannie? What's goin' on? What facts did she give you hell about?"

"Now, Selma, don't you go getting all worked up. Fannie was right. I should have had my eyes open after my children died. But I was too filled with grief and I wanted to hold everyone responsible for my unhappiness. Whoever it was in that house that day, bothering Amy will pay the price for his reckless behavior. It's just that he shouldn't have been protected."

"You betcha, he'll pay," snapped Selma. "Long overdue!"

Everyone fell quiet.

Albert was the first to speak. "I've been wondering, Marla. Do you think you could find time to come by the house and help me with some ideas? You haven't been inside before, have you? I think I'd like to put up a small fence around the back garden."

Marla turned a deep crimson. "W-well, Albert I would like to, but I can't picture what I could offer you."

Venera Di Bella Barles

# *Excerpts from the Diaries of Miss Daisy Maude Hinkle*

**1963—May**

Oh how will we make it day to day now that Ma's gone?

We found her sitting in the parlor in her rocker. I thought she would live forever. Even though we surely know Mr. Death is coming, he never knocks.

This was beginning to be one of the best years we have had in many years and now...

Rose once asked Ma if she loved her. Ma didn't answer. I'm glad I didn't ask her.

We know she had a very hard time with her own ma and pa. They were unkind to her. I would say downright selfish.

But I can say Lucille Hinkle was an odd mother. She wanted us girls to learn, however, seemed to resent when we accomplished anything. She never said it, but I think she wished that it were Rose that died, instead of Zachary. There was a big part of me that died the day he did.

I never saw Ma smile. I wonder what that would have looked like.

•

**1964—March**

I wonder what it would be like to have children of my own.

I looked through Ma's belongings today and spent time thinking about her. She didn't try to learn about the nice things of life. I wonder why she didn't want much to do with us. Violet says she was jealous.

She didn't want children—seems wrong that a mother be jealous of her daughters.

Ma talked bad about other women she hardly knew—sometimes just because they were a different nationality. She didn't like Italians. So much to learn about human nature.

Rose gave Paul Farmer a reading lesson last night. She's been able to help a lot of the men and boys with their reading and writing skills. We never see most of these men in daylight. I hope she holds up—sometimes she behaves so strange.

# Chapter 15
# Etta Mae's Drift-On Inn Motel and Diner

I awoke and lay there for a few minutes, remembering the conversation between Albert and Marla. I thought what a fine thing it would be for them to pair up. There's something about matchmaking. That union could meet so many needs. Selma looked hopeful.

I thought of Etta Mae, another woman who had endured a large dose of hardships to secure her family. Thomas Maas had told me she operated a scoop in the colliery, alongside her husband. She continued to work there, even after Ben died of gangrene from a mining accident. I was stunned by the capacity of these people to adjust to hardship. Eventually, Etta put her two children through college, left the mines, and started the motel and diner. Adversity knew its roots here.

I planned to leave in a couple of days. It was amazing how much I had learned about this region—things I had no real perceptions about. And it was amazing how much of my own wounded soul had come to light.

I rolled off the lumpy bed and peeked through the metal slats of the blinds toward the café. It was another bone-chilling, dreary day. Frost coated the edges of the single-pane window. As I glanced to my right, I saw an unusual array of trucks and cars parked in front of *Etta Mae's Drift-On Inn Motel and Diner*. It was Saturday morning, probably a good time for the local men to catch up on the news over their brew. Etta Mae always had fresh crullers.

I was surprised to see Sheriff Floyd Zimmer's green sheriff's car jammed in the middle of the lot with lights dazzling. As a rule, it was parked down the road in his marked spot in front of the one and only government building of the township. It housed the law offices, the sheriff department and city hall. His right-hand man, Officer Jack Wiley, was just pulling in. Something was not right.

Carl Fenster, his hands thrust deep into his parka, came out of the restaurant and stood near some other men. Steam drifted out between his lips and from his unlit pipe. Etta Mae followed Sheriff Zimmer. With one hand on her substantial hip, she pointed to the last room at the end of the U-shaped motel. I could hear a siren blaring from the main highway.

As much as I told myself that I shouldn't interfere in whatever was happening, I still felt the urge to know. I quickly dressed, and made my way to the hub of the community, Etta Mae's diner. The tables were all taken, so I sat at the red Formica counter. There was no retro here; everything was original 1950's. Sophie, the waitress and a niece of Etta's, acknowledged me and quietly poured a cup of coffee. The men spoke in hushed tones, careful not to catch my eye. I asked Sophie what was happening.

She replied, "There's a g-g-gal been b-b-beat up pretty bad. She a regular. She come every coupla week to s-stay on her way to see her kin in Rosedale. She always take that r-room. Nice lady. Mind her own business. See, they t-takin' her away right now." She pointed.

I wondered whether somebody had broken into the woman's room, or whether she was there with someone. Etta Mae burst through the door.

"Hiya-do, Miz Valente." She moved quickly to pick up the pot and pour refills to her customers. "Sophie fixed you up?"

I replied I was doing fine.

"I just t-told her about the hurt lady, Aunt Etta Mae," Sophie said.

"Now, don't go scarin' off my visitors. Ain't nothin' to be a' feared of. We all is goin' git to the bottom o' this. Some good-for-nothin' SOB should have his pecker shorten'd. If they ever catch that sonna-bitch, he better have his life insurance paid. Ain't nobody gonna stand for anymore of this joker's leavin's. He done do this too many times. Ugly bastard."

I couldn't believe what I was hearing. Here, in the middle of *nowhere*. I told Etta Mae that no one had mentioned these crimes before. I asked her how long had these rapes been happening here.

"*Humph!* Long enough. I guess it because dem gals ain't nobody we all knows. He's only gittin' outsiders. Been goin' on for years."

I suddenly became fearful for my own safety. I asked if the other women, who were assaulted and raped, had stayed at the motel and how did she know it was the same person doing these assaults.

"Oh, hell no, Miz Valente. This is the first time in ma place. Most been picked here and there and left shocked by the side of the road. An' he do it the same way all the time. It's too bad they like to hitchhike, but that don't give that lowlife the right to pounce on 'em. One gal was found coupla months back near dead down the road from Fannie's place. He's a sorry sonna-bitch. I better not git hold o' him. He gonna have to work pretty damn hard to mount my ass."

The ambulance left with the victim, and Officer Wiley came into the coffee bar.

"Well, there goes another one," he said in his high-pitched voice. "No tellin' how she'll recover from that beatin'."

"Got any ideas who done it, Jack?" asked Etta Mae.

"Sheriff picked up a couple of things. They got to go to forensics in Harrisburg. Can't tell nothin' for now."

She moved in front of Jack and asked, "Did he do her?"

Jack looked down to the floor and shifted his stance to his other foot. "Yeah. I'm afraid so. Pretty sorry mess."

"*Bastard.* I hear'd dem screams last night, but I thought it were a loud TV show. When she didn't come in for breakfast, somethin' told me I better check. Usually has orange juice, coffee and wheat toast. Bastard."

"Etta Mae, do you have any phone numbers for her? Maybe we can call her kinfolk."

"Hol' on a minute, I got it right chere," she mumbled as she walked to the small registration counter in the corner of the restaurant and checked the registration cards. "Sorry sonna-bitch. Who do they think they foolin'? They ain't gonna catch him. Dem girls not important enough."

She slammed a drawer, gave the information to Officer Wiley. The men in the café watched Etta Mae and held their peace.

"Patricia O'Hare. Here's a number to her ma. She not married. Just a young one. Always quiet and paid first. Told me she had a job in the next county and brung her money to home. You men ain't gonna do *anythin'* about it!"

"Now, Etta Mae, don't go jumpin' to the last sentence. I told you we're workin' on it."

Thomas Maas walked into the cafe, tipped his cap to me, and removed his cigarette. Then Carl Fenster came in behind Thomas with a man who looked like a younger version of Carl. I remembered that his son Merle was visiting him.

"Mornin', Miz Valente. Thought you already left town?" Thomas said.

His hands were raw and cracked from the cold weather, right down to his nicotine stained fingers. I inquired about his mother, Elsa. I'm sure everyone in the village had the news by now. *LSM*—Lightning Speed Marconi.

"She's doing fine. Mornin's she's cantankerous. But I've learn't to side-step her. I get her oatmeal and then I come here for my coffee. Say, did you get all you needed about them Hinkle girls?"

I responded that I seem to have enough material.

"I suppose you been hearing about the mishap. Awful shame. Awful shame."

I found myself annoyed at the word "mishap." How ungenerous of some men to downplay violence towards women. The two Fenster men sat at a table with another man, who wore a John Deere baseball cap pulled down to his eyebrows. It didn't hide the scowl on his deeply lined face.

"What she doin' by herself in a motel anyway?" the man said. "These young girls always askin' for trouble. Goin' places they shouldn't."

"What?" Etta Mae yelped. "What you mean, ole man?"

"You heard me," he smugly answered. "They ain't got no call to be out without they men."

I noticed the smirk on young Merle Fenster's face.

"You born in a cave er what, ole fool? You ain't got nary a smidgin' o' mother-wit!" Etta Mae straightened to her full six-feet. "Since when do you own the roads? I don't recall votin' for you to be judge an' jury. What give any man the right to bother any gal no matter where she be, unless'n' he invited?"

She looked at me with a raised eyebrow and then shook her short-cropped frizzed head. There wasn't going to be much in the way of converting in this exchange.

"Now, Etta Mae don't go gettin' yer knickers in a twist," another customer offered. "He was just sayin' maybe it would be a good idea if women were more careful."

"Oh, ah see, so now yer his partner. He need an interpreter? How come men can't say men need to be mindin' their ways and be mo like gentlemen?"

"I think you been hangin' too much with this big city gal, Etta Mae. She givin' you all this high'n mighty stuff?"

"Ole man, I don' need city girls to teach me. I learnt this from my mammy and that be a long time afore I knew Miz Valente. So don't be blamin' her."

"Now, you two hush," Thomas Maas said. "This ain't no way to behave. Sorry, Miz Valente, everybody's a little off."

I talked to the "John Deere man" for a few minutes, hoping to change his mind, but I knew opinions were deeply ingrained. Thomas sat down with the others. Etta Mae went back behind the counter in a huff. Sheriff Zimmer was still outdoors talking to several people while Officer Jack Wiley took photographs of the room and of Patricia O'Hare's car.

I decided to leave and visit Fannie Gottschalt. I couldn't fool myself into believing everyone approved of me.

## Venera Di Bella Barles

# *Excerpts from the Diaries of Miss Daisy Maude Hinkle*

**1967—May**

I haven't heard anything for quite a while from the publisher where I sent my *Anthology of Tears*. Maybe I should have used only my initials so they wouldn't know that I was a woman.

Still can't help to think about poor Amy. I miss her. So many losses. She said she couldn't shake that idiot man. He wouldn't keep his hands to himself. Don't know if this town will ever see the truth about her.

•

**1968—July**

Hard to make ends meet.

We will need to be more careful of our funds. It's good that Carl Fenster will lease our fields. The money will help with the old car and groceries.

Lily doesn't want much to do with us anymore, but she sends us a few dollars every once–in-awhile. She calls us 'mule-headed hermits' and says we're stuck in backward ways.

Our youngest sister doesn't understand what our lives were about. She doesn't know how much she was shielded from the misery in our home.

I only wish Violet and I could have helped Rose more…

•

**1973—July**

I've made two long-time good friends in Fannie Gottschalt and Etta Mae Jackson. They have hard edges, but you know right where you stand when you talk to them. They are doing good jobs as mothers, despite their bad luck.

It's too bad more people can't cut through their walls of lies and be more straightforward with others…just like these women.

I feel bad for Etta Mae – she's been trying to make a go of that café and motel.

People act like she has the plague. She's the only one, out of the few black families, except for Charlie Adams, that is brave enough to try and set-up another business. Charlie started his butcher shop a couple of years back and these silly folks nearly ran him out of town with their miserable ways.

What makes them think they're better than Etta and Charlie?

Sometimes I can hardly wait to get off this earth—there is so much wretched heartache.

# Chapter 16
# Faceless Women

On my drive to Fannie's gas station, I thought about the appalling situation I'd left. Something nagged at me. I wondered how hard they were trying to find the man who had torn at Patricia O'Hare. I couldn't get Etta Mae's angry exchange out of my mind.

At the café, I had witnessed the residue of male chauvinism.

A serial killer in the Northwest came to mind, and his many unsolved outrages against women. I continually felt a sense of anger that in all these years the crimes had not been solved. Not important enough? Street women? Not enough manpower? Not enough money? Not enough *blahblahblah*. But let's pull out the big guns if it's an important male celebrity.

My own sexism was showing.

Fannie's place frequently left a reassuring glow in me. Today, I yearned for her maternal wingspread of comfort. How anxious I felt. Patricia O'Hare's beating brought back harsh memories from my childhood. The overpowering helplessness and failure to stop my father's heavy hands from striking my mother. I couldn't seem to help her. Besides, Mother learned her lessons well at her own father's knee. It was easy for her to marry a bully.

I decided, instead of Fannie's place, I first needed to go back to the Hinkle house. Why I had to go, what else I had to learn, I didn't know. But the draw was strong.

I drove past Fannie's place a few miles and turned down the swollen and frozen dirt road to the Hinkle farm.

*Hello, Violet, Rose and Daisy. I'm back. I hate to bother you again today, but I feel like we are all sisters with hidden truths. Is there something you all need to tell me? You must be listening to what I am saying about myself also. You have sparked some memories that I thought I had sorted out and laid to rest. I'm quite restless with my own reflections.*

I walked to the alcove with Daisy's writings. I became lost in the small diaries. Time and dates of lives spent in overcoming perpetual tragedies; trying to understand why those that supposedly love us—also hurt us.

I read bits and pieces from the different journals. A picture was forming of Daisy and Violet and their mission in the family. They were the official caretakers of Rose and Lily. And now I understood Rose's life, unfortunately. The horror of it all was unraveling in my hands.

My dear God, I realized suddenly, Lily was Rose's baby—both Sam Hinkle's daughters.

I felt the nastiness that their father used his family in such a vile way. It was no wonder that Violet and Daisy felt enormous guilt that they were unable to protect this sister—despite the damage they had absorbed for themselves.

What a pot of worms.

Lily was Rose's baby. The unspeakable revelation cost Rose her sanity—the entire drama put a heavy toll on the family.

My hands shook from the power in the pages of these books. I would also have retreated into these walls with this tainted existence. I walked out of the alcove and into the kitchen. I stared at the area where the women were found.

*I think I understand why you decided to leave, dear sisters. Violet, and you, Daisy, had taken good care of Rose, but you were worried that she would be left alone. You weren't sure if Lily would understand or be interested in her mother, Rose. I saw that entry, in one of your last diaries, that explains things to Lily.*

*It's not my business, but I think that was the proper thing to do. Lily had a right to understand the dynamics of her family and to understand why you took the paths you did. I'm sorry your lives were so troubled—you deserved better.*

You protected your dear sister the best you could.

*"Shh, Carmela, don't move or you'll wake your sister. I'm not going to hurt you."*

*Stop it, Franco! Please, please stop!*

I remembered it all, suddenly. All in a blur, like a bad dream—but an overwhelming one. That nasty, hot summer Cousin Franco bothered me again and again. Then that day, Momma was out. He wouldn't let me go.

He was my older, visiting cousin. Cousins didn't do things like that.

The tears flowed freely. I had hidden it all from myself all those years. Not even counseling had brought it out.

I remembered the pain I felt when Gioia died. The helplessness and the loss had doubled Gina and me over. Gioia's empty bed, her scoffed little shoes, her favorite stuffed doll, with the long skinny neck where she carried it, the piece of blanket she held in her bed for security. I felt the sisterhood with my sweet flowers; Violet, Rose, Daisy and Lily.

*"Momma, why won't you believe me. Franco hurt me..."*

*"Bruta Putana, you will burn in hell for lying! Franco is going to be a priest! And you're such a little whore!"*

Bastard! He was supposed to be the hero big shot that was pure of heart, went to the seminary, and all that rot, and he was out diddling his little cousin. Quite a summer vacation getting his jollies off.

*"Let me go! Gioia is calling me—she's awake from her nap. I need to go!"*

He wouldn't let me go. I needed to go to her, but he wouldn't leave me alone—

*Gioia!*

# *Excerpts from the Diaries of Miss Daisy Maude Hinkle*

**1974—August**

I wish I could have stopped Pa from bothering Rose. It wasn't right. He got mad when I tried to stop him from going after poor little Rose. He said, "Better mind your own p's & q's, missy, afore I git the strop to ya!"

Ma didn't say anything Ma knew what was going on—but didn't do anything to stop it. It's awfully hard to love Ma.

# *Chapter 17*
# *Watchin' the Water Move On By*

"Howya-doin'?" Fannie waved as I walked into the variety store. "I'm glad you got my call. I didn't want you to leave before I said goodbye."

I was thankful no one else was there. She grabbed my arm and pulled me towards her for an embrace. I was stunned but happy with the gesture. It was the first physical touch I had received in Pine Grove Haven, other than shakings hands.

"I hope I didn't overstep myself," she said. "I feel like I knew ya all my life. You're a right gal!"

I told her it was perfectly acceptable, as a matter of fact I needed a hug today.

We spoke about the young victim found assaulted at Etta Mae's, and she told me about another girl found down the road from her business garage a while back. She said the young woman was a new customer, who had stopped to get repairs on a leaking radiator hose. While the auto was being worked on, she took a walk down the road, to pick wildflowers, intending to return in a short time.

"When she didn't come back, I told Frank, Jr. to get in his truck to look for her. He was gone a long time. When he got back he said he called Sheriff Zimmer and they took her over to Doc Hanford's 'cause she was pretty banged up. Frank, Jr. said he thinks she was, you know, bothered like that. He said he found her off the highway, she was pretty messed up, just like them other gals. Sheriff questioned Frank, Jr. a bit."

I asked Fannie if she felt the sheriff and his men were working to find the man.

"I'm guessin' they are, but I can't see a damn thing they doin'. Maybe they waitin' for somebody to die. They asked Frank, Jr. questions then released him, like I said. *Humph,* I guess they figure it's just a dang woman." Fannie lit a cigarette and straightened her blouse and sweater, then stared out of the steam-covered window. "They say they got their eye on Clive Mooney, a real piece o'God's work. Funny stuff going on for years and nobody is claimin' responsibility."

I remembered the man I saw the second day of my arrival. He stood on the church grounds gazing at me with fixed, cold eyes. He was strongly built, a De Niro-type, he couldn't be over sixty. I shivered when I thought of him. I couldn't shake that feeling that there was more about him than I understood.

Instead of writing a simple novel, I felt like an investigator researching a true crime thriller. I had so many new questions now, since this morning. At the rate I was going, I'd never be able to leave. I asked her to tell me a little more about who this De Niro-type was.

"Clive's an odd one, and I can't tell if he's the sort to do that kind of thing. Everyone knows him here in Pine Grove Haven. Does odd jobs for folks, in between beer deliveries. Used to help the Hinkle girls with repairs, but it's no wonder he turned out so mean. He's been in trouble ever since he born. A long time, even afore the days I bartended. Sometimes he can be as sweet as honey and other times he has a real nasty streak."

Fannie moved her hands and arms widely. Minnie, the cat, kept an eye on her.

"His mother was a hellcat on wheels an' a number-one whore. Do just anythin' for whiskey. That young buck had just about every bone in his body turned to sawdust by her an' her boyfriends. He saw everythin' afore he left her knee. I'm guessin' he had enough misery."

She took quick puffs and then inhaled deeply. "Everythin's got its price. I supposin' we look like some pretty bad low-lifers to you." She wiped the same area of the counter over and over with a grimy rag.

Fannie Gottschalt was embarrassed.

I reassured her that this was a small piece of what humankind is, with all its flaws. No town escapes the sad portraits of life.

She nodded in agreement. "You're right, I know." She came around to the front of the showcase, stood a few seconds looking me over. "We got to keep in touch when you leave, ya hear? Don't forget to give me your address, now. Say, that's one pretty scarf around your neck."

I looked at her eyes; even the dead one revealed need. I took the scarf off, put it around her throat, and gave her a hug.

"What? What you doin', Carmela?" Fannie pulled away from me. "This ain't right!"

I insisted she take it to remember me by.

"Well, I never. I ain't never had a present from a stranger. My, my, you're a fine lady."

We sat quietly talking for a few minutes, reviewing what had happened these last several weeks. I trusted her. She was the kind of woman I would have sought out back home.

I found it eye-opening how many of these people had personalities similar to the friends and families I grew up with. Fannie was so much like a friend of mine, a plainspoken, warm, woman who could easily read people's psyches. I knew her for a fleeting moment in my life, but she spread her magical ways forever in me.

"Are you missing your friends? I supposin' they smart like you." She brushed the scarf with her hand lightly. "One of these days I got to get the heck out of here an' travel a little 'afore I pack it in. Frank, Jr. said he'd fix up that ole Toyota. He said he could take care of the shop for us, iff'n I wanted to do a little sight-seein'. My daughter, Robyn Lee, said she could take a leave from her job for a while an' help run the store. Frank, Jr. kin run the car shop. I ain't been further then Philly." Fannie buttoned her sweater, pushed her drab, dyed hair behind her ear, and lit another cigarette. "Worked there for about six months, but it were hard on my kids. Never knowin' where the next buck would come from."

Fannie sounded like my father. Always yearning for better.

Customers came in to purchase a few sundries and pay for gas. I watched as this warrior woman went about the routine of following the laws of survival. She didn't whine or complain.

When she was through, she walked to the pot-bellied stove and tossed in another log. If I lived here, I could see that this haunt would be an oasis of consolation. It brought to mind the different areas of peaceful retreats in my life: sharing time with the family in the backroom of my grandfather's grocery store, sitting around the iron wood-stove; sitting near a window in the attic listening to the rain on the slate roof; sitting in a daze, curled up on the overstuffed living room chair, making patterns on the fabric's cut velvet design while my parents battled.

"You look lost in your head. Somethin' on your mind?"

I told her my thoughts.

"For me it was when me 'n my friend picked and ate apples by the crick, watchin' the water move on by. That's where we learnt to read. We got some ole *Saturday Evening Posts* from the barbershop, an' little by little we figured out how to read what was under the pictures. But most times, I had to bring in money for my folks. Say, Carmela, are ya gonna write your book when ya get back home?"

I told her I most likely would, but I wasn't sure how I would go about it.

"I ain't had much time to write anythin' but signin' my name on bills an' checks," she said. "It's a whole 'nother world—writin', drawin', an all that stuff. I reckon' some of us have to be the appreciators."

She looked at me pensively. I replied that her innate capabilities had taken her far and that her qualities most certainly surpassed some well-educated citizens of the planet. I reminded her that she survived a difficult life of trying to protect, shelter, feed, and advance her family with very little support. No one starved for lack of love around her.

"*Humph!* I'm guessin' you're right there. Never quite thought of it that way. You'll be leavin' soon?"

I told her my plane would leave on Monday afternoon. I asked her if she felt there was anyone else in the village that could flesh out my story, or add information to my findings. I confided some of the details of my discoveries, but not the finding of the penknife and the missing diary. I still wanted to hear if anyone would bring these up in conversation.

But, now, there was something new. Clive Mooney. The finding of the penknife with the engraved initials *CM* and Daisy's missing diary confirmed my beliefs of what happened to Amy on that disastrous day. I was intrigued by the possibility that he might also be the one committing the assaults. Uneasiness simmered through me. I asked Fannie if my views were valid.

"Well, now, Carmela, you're a regular Ellery Queen, ain't cha?"

I laughed at being identified with the old detective.

"You sure seem to be on the right track. What makes me so dang fumin' is how well that sonna-bitch seems protected from bein' exposed."

I remembered Daisy's notes.

## Venera Di Bella Barles

# *Excerpts from the Diaries of Miss Daisy Maude Hinkle*

**1975—February**

What could we have done, short of killing our father, to have prevented him from molesting Rose? Pa swore us to secrecy. Lily still does not know who her real mother is. Of course Ma was no help—turned her head the other way and blamed Rose.

Sometimes days go by and we don't see a single soul.

Most homes have telephones, but Pa said we didn't need one. So, now, even after all these years since his death he can still control our heads. What was it about him that we didn't use our own heads?

Our pipes froze and busted yesterday morning. The house is pretty old and something is always breaking.

Violet is terribly upset. I dislike it when she loses patience. Her screeching bothers Rose and me. I know she hates to ask for help. She says we should be able to take care of everything ourselves. I have tried to convince her that maybe we should get a telephone for emergencies. It's hard for her to understand that we're not spring chickens any longer.

Thank goodness for Clive Mooney and Carl Fenster dropping by. They have helped quite a bit.

•

**1980—July**

I saw John Schoen in town today. We chatted for quite some time. What a dear gentle man. He showed me a few pages of his writings from a notebook. He writes like a regular Steinbeck. He seems able to capture the hard-luck tales of the mines. John said that he has been speaking for years to a lot of old miners to gather the information. He asked if I would be willing to edit his work. I told him I'd be glad to help him.

# *Chapter 18*
# *Intermezzo*

Fannie and I spent most of the morning together. My plans were to see a few more folks that day, then maybe make another visit to the Hinkle house. I also wanted to revisit the graveyard to take some photographs. The day in the cemetery had been profoundly indelible. It was there where I had most felt the poignancy and richness of this community.

Also, I needed to say my goodbyes to the people of the valley. Most likely I would see several of them tomorrow, Sunday, at the Pine Grove Haven Church of God. It was remarkable how many unique folks I had met. I was going to miss many of them. I surprised myself with my own level of intimacy.

Leaving them reminded me of when I was young and the numerous times I moved with my parents—always losing those temporary friends along the way—just enough time to connect, but lacking development of emotional ties. Maybe, that was why I was a loner most of my life, cutting my own paths, making sure that intimacy was the last requirement for acquaintances; easier to stop the bleeds.

In many ways this was a town of loners. The Hinkle women had become hermits, but aren't many of us city dwellers close to this description? Hermits—living in our closed-off homes, apartments, and offices?

It was true that Daisy Hinkle, the chronicler, kept in touch with her neighbors by archiving their personal facts. Her profiles charted each of their lives with Daisy's brand of statistics garnered from newspaper clippings of births, weddings, and deaths. She did an exhaustive study of people's lives, often with an analysis consisting of her suspicions. Then she wove the particulars into her many fictional tales.

In all of Daisy's writings, except for her diaries, I found little about her family. There were a few facts about her parents, but not much concerning her sisters. In truth, most came from the personal journals. I'd learned less about the Hinkles than about everyone in Pine Grove Haven.

In their younger years, they were activists, in step with the times by reaching out to make a difference, but as their time wore on, they retreated. Their parents left their mark on them, which contributed to their pain. I'm sure the struggle was occasionally dramatic for the elderly women. Their lives came with sharp teeth.

The events of the last few days had been unsettling. I was uncomfortable as I lay in my bed that night, thinking of the criminal attack on Patricia O'Hare, who had been down a few rooms from mine. I listened to the wind wailing outdoors. I shivered and got out of bed to put a straight chair under the doorknob. Funny how fear builds irrational cells in our brains.

Large cities have had major crimes happening with great regularity, but this wasn't supposed to happen here in this quiet, almost abandoned community tucked away in these scarred hills.

I tossed about, my thoughts not letting me sleep, and reflected about the townsfolk who had befriended me: Elsa Maas had strange inflexible ways, yet she revealed her humanitarian traits, taking care of babies and mothers, speaking up when she didn't approve of misconduct. Rock-solid Selma and her gentle daughter Marla tried to hold their lives together with three little girls to raise. Carl Fenster, a lonely, hard working man, feeling responsible for the deaths of the Hinkle women. Fannie Gottshalt, as strong as they come, using every piece of wit and courage to keep her family from the wolf, and still guiding her existence with hard work. Etta Mae Jackson, who'd had the pluck to break the gender and racial walls, becoming a miner alongside her husband, while continuing to voice a stand against injustice. Nell Miller was bent to a lifetime of pain with a self-centered hypocrite; what did Pastor Cyrus Miller's congregation get from his brand of twaddle? Thomas Maas, a miner, gave his skills to the community as a loyal fire-fighter-rescuer, dedicating years to his mother. And then there was Albert Schoen and his family, still attempting to go forward with the fragments of their tragic lives.

Truly, these were noble people. I had learned much from them. I could never more think the way I had when I first drove into Pine Grove Haven. How could I have misjudged these proud citizens? Never did I believe that they could show me new feelings and new ways of thinking.

After I said my goodbyes at the church, I had a pleasant Sunday dinner with Fannie and Frank, Jr. We promised to stay in touch.

•

I left early Monday morning to drive my rental back to the airport in Baltimore. The roads were icy, and the semi-trailers rolling down the highway at break-neck speed adding extra effort to my steering.

As I sat on the plane bound for Seattle, I thought I had left many of the unsettled issues back in the small mining village. But I'd found much more than I'd come looking for.

I imagined the scene with Amy Schoen and Clive Mooney. Fannie said that day of the twins' death; Clive had been to the house to fix some plumbing. He may have presumed that, since she was alone, he could make a little time with her. But when Amy heard her little son's desperate cry for help, Amy had struggled frantically to extricate herself from Clive's insistent grip, and when she escaped, he left quickly.

In my mind, I had sorted out the events and made my conclusions. It was an eye-opening couple of weeks. The layers of this community had yielded a diverse and complicated set of rules. The most revealing was how alike we were.

**Venera Di Bella Barles**

# *Excerpts from the Diaries of Miss Daisy Maude Hinkle*

**1985—February**

I often think of how my life will end. I don't know if I could go on without my sisters. What do our lives mean? What could we have accomplished differently?

Violet used to say she wished she could have been a librarian. Rose used to sing when she was a girl. Sweet voice, but shy to let anyone listen. I would have loved seeing more of my writings in print. And Lily, being the only one married, knows what having a child is like, except for Rose. Lily's a good girl, but a little bent that we don't see things like she does. She says we're backward. Maybe, we are. I think it's too harsh out there in the world.

The winters are getting more difficult. My eyes are not seeing as well.

# *Chapter 19*
# *They Pine an' Die Just Like Us*

Not long after I returned, I started my new novel. The events of those weeks in Pine Grove Haven had changed me in many ways. As I begun to write, I realized the book was becoming semi-auto-biographical. I drew parallels with my own daily life to the people of that small unremarkable community. They were alive in my thoughts.

I called Fannie every couple of months. Her phone replies were typically to the point.

"Carmela, I finally saw my daughter Mary Lee's place and stayed at her real fancy Bed and Breakfast. It was so full of life, clean, and green; I'd say 'fit for a queen'. Not gray like Pine Grove Haven. Frank, Jr. and Robyn Lee, my other daughter, took care of the shop for me. If it tweren't for you, I most likely wouldn't of gone."

Fannie thanked me for the encouragement, and I told her

that's what friendship was all about.

"I'm findin' that out. Just last week Elsa Maas asked about you. Funny duck. She said she liked you and hoped you would come back to see us here. She liked your spunk."

I told Fannie that I thought Elsa was a surprising woman with many facets to her personality. It took a bit to warm up to her, but after I understood her better, we hit it off just fine.

"Ha! You can stick a feather in your cap for that. It ain't often that she gathers new friends, but she is trustworthy. No BS there!"

I thought a few minutes and then told her about the pocketknife I'd found at the Hinkle home. I revealed I had meant to give it to her before I left. I was hoping that she could return it to Clive Mooney.

She was understandably astonished.

"What? You say you found it at the house. What was he doin' there? Tryin' to steal what little was left?"

I also told her about one of Daisy's missing diaries.

"That sonna-bitch! I'll bet he was lookin' for somethin'. I swear. You know that Sheriff ain't arrested Clive yet. It's a good thing nothin' else has happened since they found that girl in Etta Mae's motel. One of these days, it's all gonna blow up in that viper's face. You wait. I can't figure out what he was doing with Daisy's diary. That's mighty strange. I wonder what that was all about."

The exasperation in her voice reminded me of my short stay in the complicated town. I was glad to be away from those worries. I told her not to fret so, that evil would meet its comeuppance and things would soon be sorted out.

"You're right there. It's just that when you're gettin' old, you don't have patience for this crap!"

I asked what the news was in the rest of the valley.

"Well, now, let's see, it looks like Albert asked Selma's daughter, Marla, to marry him. She is just so happy and those little girls are jumpin' out of their skin, exceptin' for the older one, Katy; she suddenly got quiet. Guess she thought she wasn't doin' right by her pa to jump into another daddy's arms. Always somethin' isn't it, Carmela?"

I agreed, but I told her how thrilled I felt at the news.

"Yeah, it do feel good. Albert said they was gonna move into his old place. Made that house right pretty. Has a sturdy picket fence 'round the property to look after Marla's children. Them little girls sure like that house."

I asked Fannie if the Hinkle dwelling was still empty.

"Well, now, Lily Hinkle, you know, Daisy's younger sister, finally came to clear out some of the family goods. That place needs some good folks in there to bring it back to life. Houses are like people—if you don't take care of them, they pine an' die, just like us. By the way, Lily said she was thinkin' of publishin' some of her sister's stories. Daisy must be beamin' 'neath that dirt!"

My eyes blurred with tears, and I had a lump in my throat when I heard this. I told Fannie how pleased I was to hear that. Daisy had yearned for that honor. I said that I would mail the knife to her for Clive.

"I hate to tell you where I'd like to put that thing!"

I told her to calm her thoughts. We ended on a good note when I conveyed to her that the next time I came to visit my daughter in Maryland, I most likely would come by and spend a day or two in Pine Grove Haven.

"Now you're talkin'. I'll polish-up the sign out front."

## *Excerpts from the Diaries of Miss Daisy Maude Hinkle*

**1986—January**

Marla, Selma's daughter, and her husband Jake had their third girl—named her Lizzy.

Jake's on the road a lot driving those big rig trucks. He's a good man – studies geology in Harrisburg. He says he wants to get a better job. That would be good for them all. Marla and he are a good quality pair.

Violet's bad hip is acting up. We need to go to town to get some help. But Violet can hardly drive anymore. All three of us are ailing. It's a nuisance having folks paying mind to our ills. Rose is so out of sorts. She mostly lives in the past now.

It helps to have Jack's two boys deliver food to us.

•

**1986—February**

Carl's son, Merle, came to visit his pa this week, from Minneapolis. I have never been there. It seems like I've never been anywhere except as far as Harrisburg. Went there several times when Dora and I fought for the miners—so long ago. Dora Fenster was a scrappy one.

Merle is a strange boy. He appears restless. I do wonder what he does with himself up there in that big city. Carl's not happy with him for not settling down.

•

**1986—March**

John said that Albert is planning to move back to Pine Grove Haven. He may fix up his old cottage. It's been empty for several months, since Fred Farnsworth died.

Was a time when Fred and I spoke the loudest in the valley for the workers. He was a brave and honorable man. He pushed through some significant changes for the laborers. I'll always remember how he was able to get the G-men to look into the abuses the company guards and bosses were doing to the women and stealing right under our noses.

•

**1986—April**

Selma told me that Sheriff Floyd and Officer Jack, Jim Wiley's youngest, are pretty busy lately. Fannie says they should get help with the number of assaults.

The women aren't local – I guess just traveling through.

When times get hard, men get desperate. They seem to lose themselves in anger—the only emotion they allow themselves.

# Chapter 20
# Theories, Conjectures, and Truths

At Christmas, I received a card from Fannie with a short note and a newspaper clipping. It choked me up to read the news. The article said that a Minneapolis man was placed under arrest for a series of previously unsolved rapes. I had difficulty accepting what I read. It was discovered many of the offenses had taken place over a long period of time in and around a small town in Pennsylvania. Fannie wrote that Merle Fenster admitted that many of the offenses were committed when he visited his father.

I dropped the card, gasped, and felt a deep sadness for Carl Fenster. Had God set up this community as a model for the world's maladies?

Fannie also wrote that since Sheriff Zimmer had arrested Clive Mooney, he would now be cleared of the criminal assault charges. Clive proved he wasn't in the township at the time of the rapes.

So much for theories. It threw a completely new light on my conclusions. How easy it was for me to jump to them. I wanted to package everything. How many people are burned by unsubstantiated judgments?

I made a phone call to Fannie early in January.

"Well, I'll be! Carmela, it's so good to hear your voice. Yes, yes, I'm doin' as well as I can. Got a little rheumatism in that hip and knee 'o mine, but can't spend too much time complainin'. Frank, Jr. decided to go to college in Philly, an' he's gonna stay with his sister, Melissa Ann. You remember, she's my deaf daughter that teaches them hard o' hearin' babies. I'm gonna miss him terribly."

I asked her how she was going to manage the garage without Frank, Jr.

"It's damn lonely now that the last of my kids are gone." There was a long deep sigh and then silence. "I'm ok. I'm ok. Just thinkin' about it all. My friend, Dewey, is helpin' for now. His dad finally died a month ago. Was sick a stretch. Carpentry was a little slow, so I took Dewey on in the garage. He also knows a fair amount about cars an' trucks. Not much he don't know about. I don't know if I got enough business to keep him on."

Fannie asked how I was and if I had finished the book. I told her I was nearly done with the first draft and that my life had changed since my visit to Pine Grove Haven. I was happy that I was closer to my children, sister, and family. I had decided not to put off things that I felt were important to me. Life was too precious.

"Now, you're talkin'. You taught me that for cryin' out loud. What else you got up your sleeve?"

I laughed. She could read people. I told her I had met

someone quite nice and that we were spending a great deal of time together. He was a good friend of my sister, divorced for a few years with grown married children. My daughters were friends with his family. I also told her he has a wiry dog named Ollie, a barker, but cute. Fannie was elated at the news.

"I knew it. Ya don't have any business livin' alone."

I gave it right back to her. I said, "What about Fannie getting a little romance in her life?"

"What? Ain't nobody here I need to get lovey-dovey with. But I been thinkin' someday I'm just gonna sell this place and move closer to my kids. Get me some teeth and a new hair bob. I still got sap in these veins; I just have to unplug 'em. I might just get me to that island you live on near Seattle. Won't you be a surprised chicken?"

We both had a good laugh at our plans. It was energizing and so much better than discussing death. But I did want to ask her how Carl Fenster was doing.

"He's just one poor skunk. Now, with his dang son, Merle, in prison in Minneapolis, he's lonelier than ever. He told me the other day that he sure is glad his wife, Dora, wasn't alive for all this miserable news. People don't much talk to him about it. Except for Thomas. Some ignorant ones just dropped him like a hot potato—like he was the one that committed those rapes. His other two kids hardly make it out to see him. Livin' sure kicks you in the butt, don't it?"

I agreed there certainly were enough boulders in our paths.

"Thomas Maas and Carl meet for coffee and crullers just about everyday at Etta Mae's. At least he has good friends there. A body only needs one good friend. Etta Mae fixes him a special meal every few days. And Satin is good company."

I marveled at the many strong relationships.

"Yeah, I'll say. Lotta good folks—if you just give them a

chance. Say, Carmela, I wanted to ask you about the Hinkle girls. You got a clear head. What did you ever figure out why they decided to throw in the sponge? I mean, what came over them? I been feelin' bad for a spell thinkin' about how their lives ended. I wished that I hadn't been so busy with my own junk, and had paid better attention to what was happenin' with them. The town was gettin' used to not seein' or hearin' anythin' about them. Stupid, dumb loss. We were all to blame."

I didn't see the need to remind her of their obvious depression, loneliness and the feeling that they were a burden to their friends. My own feeling was they felt abandoned by family, especially by their sister, Lily.

I told her that she couldn't take care of the world – even though she thought she had to. I was sure there were many reasons that helped make their decision.

"*Aahuh.* Maybe that's how they'll find me someday."

I replied I didn't think so. She was too much a survivor, and she had given her children the right tools to know how to pay back their mother with loving care.

"Well, that sounds ok. I don't want to rush things, you understand. I'll wait my turn," she said with a snigger. "It looks like I'm going to have to hang up for now. I got me some customers comin' in. I can't tell you how much I enjoy chattin' with you. You're like a long lost sister."

I told her it was wonderful speaking with her and I promised again that I would try to make a trip to see her when I came out to the east coast to visit my daughter.

"I'm countin' on you."

## *Excerpts from the Diaries of Miss Daisy Maude Hinkle*

**1986—October**

Carl won't be plowing the fields any longer. Says he's terribly sorry, but there isn't any money in it for him. People have been kind to us. We're just getting too old. We can't take care of ourselves the way we used to. Rose is so frail and Violet can hardly walk or hear and she's scarcely eating.

•

**1986—November**

We can't drive the car in winter any longer—roads are not safe. Doesn't seem like there is much left for us. We're just taking up space. Tomorrow morning I need to talk with Violet.

**1986—December**

Violet and I talked again this morning. Tomorrow will be New Year's Eve.

I have lived eighty-eight years, Violet ninety-two and Rose eighty-three—truly a lifetime. We had two hundred and sixty-three years between us to sort it all out.

Zachary will have been gone sixty-seven years tomorrow. It is as if I just heard of his death.

I haven't seen fox for a while. I wonder if animals make decisions to change the direction of their lives?

I never thought I'd end up this forlorn and cut-off from folks. I thought all would be so different these many years. I worked so hard to make the changes and take the chances of this mortal life, but it was a mere drop in the bucket.

I wanted so to believe that my parents were perfect. If we had lived on top of the shale, could we have seen further into the distance? Could we then have experienced life with another meaning?

Ma covered her eyes to the pain in her family, but she brought her own ache with her. Pa worked himself to death and found relief in our poor Rose. Did he not know the damage he brought upon our heads? I know I speak of it often, but I can't settle with it.

All our lives, it seems death was the forerunner and dictator of dreams. The mines swallowed men whole and left their families scrambling like ants.

Our sweet little Rose seems to understand what we must do. We have all agreed. Tonight we will use up our wood.

# Chapter 21
# And It Came to Pass...

I returned the following spring to the community situated between "hollers and patches." It was a friendlier image than the bitter one of my first winter stay.

The creeks ran swiftly and the trees, with their revived gray-white bark, had new, tender leaves. Wildflowers pushed through the still brown grasses, as baby birds chirped their plea for nourishment. A fox, with its pointed snout and ears upright, stopped to check before leaving its lair.

I drove past *Etta Mae's Drift-On Inn Motel and Diner* and saw Sheriff Zimmer's car parked along side the familiar worn-out trucks. Except for the change of season, time here seemed to have stood still. I felt strange, the same emotion I had the first time I came to Pine Grove Haven—my sense that nothing could possibly happen in a town like this. But now I knew differently.

I drove through the settlement slowly to appreciate the layout of the area in its new spring vestments. A few pastel-colored gardens were coming to life against the faded houses. Even Carl Fenster's fields had freshly turned black soil. I was glad to see that he still worked at his chores, in spite of everything, but I felt a pang for him. Stigmas last long. I remembered how my marriage stigmatized the family. In my father's eyes I had committed the ultimate disgrace: marriage without his permission, marriage outside his culture and religion. A moment's decision—a lifetime to mend and ponder.

Albert's now-cheerful cottage, sitting by Black Creek, came into sight, with shutters, flower-boxes, and a picket fence surrounding the entire property. I felt delight as I viewed the long-overdue salve coating the tragic home. Maybe a special benevolence had finally come to Albert and Marla.

I rolled my car into Fannie's parking lot and sat for a minute remembering the winter's cold display of this run-down building with its last shards of paint clinging to several clapboards. I had not talked to Fannie since the last phone call. I told her then that I would be away on business and vacation and that I would call her when I returned. This would be a surprise visit.

I walked to the entry and admired the new wood screen door. Wasps swarmed over my head as I neared their nest, tucked into the eaves. I cautiously and swiftly moved through the door. Fannie was deeply engrossed in a paperback as I entered. She looked up and peered over her magnifiers.

"Well I'll be danged! Carmela, you're a sight for this one-good eye! I'll be danged! I ain't talked to you for a while. Why didn't you let me know you were comin'?"

She looked first rate. Her hair was cut short and dyed a nice shade of auburn. Fannie had also lost weight and had engaged some new grooming techniques that removed ten years from her face and body. She came around the counter and gave me a long bear hug.

"Well, I'll be! You look years younger. I was just thinkin' of calling you."

I quickly returned the compliment, still amazed at her metamorphosis.

"I'm gonna have me some new teeth soon. How long can you stay? I hope you'll stay around for a while."

I told her I could stay the night, but would have to take off late tomorrow afternoon. I accepted and thanked her for her hospitality. I insisted on paying.

"Have you lost your mind? How often do you suppose I get this kind of company? No, *sireeee*. You and me is got history now. We as good as kin."

The contented look on her face said it all. She was a glorious woman. I was lucky to have gathered some outstanding people in my life, folks who taught me lessons I didn't even know I needed to learn.

She was ready to give me a sandwich, but I said I wasn't hungry. I asked how her new man, Dewey, was working out.

She blushed. "He's an honest to goodness joy to be with. He's so kind and considerate. Looks after me as if I were kin. I think he likes to be here with me. He's had nothin' but misery at his house. First, it was his ma. She died two years ago with lung cancer. And then his pa died this past year. He had lung disease much longer. We all thought he'd go before his wife. Dewey's sister, Jessie, married not long after their pa died." Fannie opened the door to the garage. "Hey, Dewey, take a break and c'mon in here. I want you to meet someone."

She turned back to me. "We fixed up a part of the shop for his furniture buildin'. He's so good at that. He's sold a few pieces since he moved in. Dewey's getting more business 'cause people travelin' can see our advertising signs better on this highway. Works on the automotive stuff for me in between."

Dewey came in from the shop. He looked less gaunt and had filled out attractively since I last saw him. He had a decided spring to his step. I could see he wasn't as young as I had thought, but had pleasing features. He walked over to Fannie's side. She looked radiant as she took two cigarettes out of the package that was in her pocket. Dewey rushed to light one for her and then lit his. There was a comfortable bond between them.

"You recall Ms. Carmela Valente, don't you?"

"Yes. How ya doin'?" When he removed his baseball cap to greet me his long wavy brown hair fell to his shoulders. He extended his hand. "Excuse me, my hands aren't too clean. I remember seein' you in Fannie's store. That was before my pa died."

I said I recalled his visit. I gave him my sympathies.

"Thank you. He'd been sick a long time. It was good not to see him suffer any more. You gals want some coffee?"

He set up three cups and started to pour, before I could answer. We talked about his knowledge of cars and his skill with woodcraft. I told him my father was a wood-carver and carpenter. I asked him how he liked working for Fannie.

"She's brought me back to life. I can't say anything better than that. I sold a maple coffee table yesterday."

Fannie jumped in to say, "If it weren't for Dewey, my shop would have hit the skids. He's able to work on all kinds of machinery, so that brings in a lot more business." She tried hard to play down the moment.

I looked at them both as I drank my coffee. I could not mistake what I saw. That undeniable element of love and companionship had laced two hearts.

Dewey stood up. "Well, Carmela, it was good to finally meet you. Fannie's been talkin' up a storm about you. I got to get back to work now, but I hope we see you again soon."

"Dewey," Fannie said, "Carmela is going to stay the night and have dinner with us. We'll eat around six-thirty."

"I'll be all shined up by then. Want me to start the meal?"

"Thanks, but I have it all figured out. You can help clean up if you don't mind."

"You know I don't." Walking out to the auto shop, he yelled back, "She makes a mean meal, Carmela."

Fannie looked at my face. "I guess you're wondering what that's all about."

I smiled.

"That's what I like about you—there's no pullin' punches with you. I remember somethin' Will Rogers once said: 'If you find yerself in a hole, the first thin' to do is stop diggin'.'"

I laughed and shook my head at her astuteness.

After dinner, Dewey cleared the table and we launched right into reports of our families and, of course, Pine Grove Haven. We spoke of the obvious news of Merle Fenster's arrest.

Fannie leaned forward. "That was a shocker for the whole town. Folks were just bowled over with the news. Poor Carl. He didn't need this."

I then remembered I had brought the penknife with me. I handed it to her and asked if she would return it to Clive. She looked it over disbelievingly.

Dewey reacted immediately. "What? This here ain't Clive's."

Fannie's jaw tightened. "This belongs to that miserable

piece o' crap, the Reverend Cyrus Miller. He used to come in the store, sit at the tables, and clean his nails with it."

My mouth fell open. I couldn't respond. My mind was swimming with new questions. C. M., Cyrus Miller not Clive Mooney?

After my shock, I discussed with Fannie my theory of the man who was with Amy on the day her children died. Also, I told her that a diary had been taken from the Hinkle house.

•

The next morning, I arose early and announced that I personally would deliver the penknife to the clergyman.

Fannie looked a little worried as she poured coffee for me. She said, "You're pretty upset and are likely to blow your stack. So, I'm comin' with you."

I told her I could handle the job, but if she wanted to join me that would be fine.

I called up Nell Miller, who was elated I was back for a visit, and I asked if I could drop by to see the Reverend Miller.

During the drive over, Fannie was uncharacteristically silent.

Nell answered the door and was surprised that Fannie was also standing at the threshold. Nell Miller held my hand with both of hers. She was tense as if she could sense my task. Reverend Miller was sitting in his wing chair as Nell led us into the living room.

The Reverend spoke, "Well, well, well, what do we have here? Mrs. Carmela Valente and Mrs. Fannie Gottschalt. What brings you back to these parts, Miz Valente? This looks like a mighty important business call. Am I right?" He crossed his legs and assumed a commanding posture. "Sit down. What's on your mind?"

"Well, Reverend," I began, "I will be leaving later this afternoon, but I needed to clear-up a matter with you first."

"With me?"

Nell moved to the other side of the room.

"I've come to return something of yours and I'm sure you will know where you misplaced it." I felt calm as I spoke. I had trepidations on the drive over that I might not be able to face him, but something seemed to anchor me and my ability to pull my thoughts together came into play.

"You have somethin' of mine? Can't be very important or I would have missed it."

I reached into my pocket, withdrew the penknife and showed it to him. "I thought you might be missing this by now."

"Well, I'll be. Yes, I always keep it with me and I must have lost it a while back. Isn't that nice of you to return this."

He began to get up to retrieve the knife.

"Not quite yet, Reverend Miller. Not until you can tell us why I found this in the Hinkle house and why all the papers and journals had been searched through. And there is one other thing..."

"What gives you the right to question me in that tone of voice—you are pushing yourself a bit far. Besides our doin's are our doin's, am I right, Fannie?" He didn't wait for her answer. "I cannot believe your interference into our lives here in Pine Grove Haven. So what if I lost my knife. What does that have to do with you?"

He stood up. His eyes bulged with fury.

I stood up and moved forward. "I'll be glad to tell you. You were a very busy man, weren't you? You even managed to take one of Daisy's diaries that day you lost your knife. These women may not be fully aware of your shenanigans, but you can't fool everyone. You were the man who was in the house with Amy the day her children died and you and I both know that is the truth. All these years you've spent playing a wicked game with God's collar."

*"Get away, Franco. I'm supposed to be watching my little sister! My father will kill me if he finds out what you're doing."*

"You knew you were in trouble when I told you Daisy was writing all these happenings down. Amy told Daisy what took place and Daisy put it into that journal. That's why you stole the book. You watched Amy die, because you weren't honorable to step forward and clear her name."

"I have no book and give me back that knife. You're one crazy woman!" He lunged for the knife.

I pulled the knife back. He immediately raised his hand in a strike position. "Do you think you can deal with me like you have treated Nell all this time? You have bullied everyone in your path." I felt like I was shouting at my father for all the years of beatings he doled out to the family. "You used your position of veneration and authority to have your way."

Cyrus Miller was bright crimson and gasping for breath.

Nell left the room and returned with the lavender journal with the year "1952" in the lower back cover. "Is this the book, Carmela? I found it one day under the car seat."

"Exactly, Nell. Exactly," I said.

Cyrus Miller came towards me with both hands outstretched. He was going for my neck. I was ready for him. "You'd like to add me to your list of victims, wouldn't you?"

"You're a vicious bitch!" His hands were around my throat—pressing. I struggled to break his hold with every ounce of strength. His face became a demon mask. My breath was fading. I could feel my head getting lighter. Fannie had come behind him and was pulling at his pants and jacket. When suddenly, I felt his fingers loosening and I regained a bit of wind. I looked down and saw the reverend on the floor, collapsed at my feet. His wife Nell had struck his head with an iron doorstop. A pool of blood was gathering.

"Oh, my God, Nell," I shrieked. "Did you kill him?"

Nell stood lifeless. The turn of events were overpowering. I put my hands to my face, not able to speak.

Fannie called the EMTs.

Then, Nell, Fannie, and I sat holding hands quietly until help arrived.

After the ambulance departed, the sheriff and his team took down the reports from the three of us, we then left for Fannie's store.

When we got to the gas station, Fannie spoke first to Dewey. She told him the whole story as it unfolded at the Miller's house.

Dewey asked, "Are they gonna' arrest anybody?"

"Naw. It don't look like the Sheriff is goin' to put any charges on us."

"I wonder how bad he's hurt and if he'll die?" he asked.

"Don't know yet. But it's a damn shame he didn't. I heard he's as good as dead. Can't talk or walk. But we still don't know how he'll turn out."

"He could be out of commission for a long time," I said.

"Yeah, but," Dewey said, "the only bad thing is that most likely Nell will be stuck takin' care of that puke. At least he can't whack her around now. Sorry excuse for a man."

"I wished you could have seen Carmela in action, Dewey. She held her ground without backing off the Reverend."

I looked at her through a haze of emotions, unable to react to all that I heard.

"You okay?"

I nodded and said, "I feel sorry for Clive. All these years that people were suspicious of him. It just wasn't fair. And has anyone told Albert?"

"We didn't need to. Everybody put two and two together. Word moves around like lightning.'"

I reminded Fannie how angry Albert was. "Remember, he vowed to find whoever was in the house with Amy. That probably was the reason she protected Miller, afraid of her husband's rash behavior."

"Yeah, I know, but he ain't gonna do nothin'." She looked out of the window then grabbed my hand tightly. "He's too happy now to have revenge in his heart. We all need to move on."

"I guess it is better that way, Fannie," I replied. "I also settled a few things for myself today."

The beginning…

# PINE GROVE HAVENS WHO'S WHO, 1988

## VACENTE

| | |
|---|---|
| Carmela, (age 65) | Born 1923 |
| Widowed for ten years. | |
| Has 2 daughters/3 grandchildren | |
| Gina (age 62), sister | Born 1926 |
| Gioia, sister | 1928-1931 |
| Salvatore, Carmela's father | |
| Antonietta, Carmela's mother | |

## FENSTER

| | |
|---|---|
| Carl, father (age 76) | Born 1912 |
| Dora, mother | 1912-1986 (died at 73) |
| Older son (age 58) | 1930 |
| Daughter (age 56) | 1932 |
| Merle, son (age 49) | 1939 |

## GOTTSCHACT

| | |
|---|---|
| Fannie (age 59) | 1929 |
| Frank, Jr. (age 39) | 1949, youngest child |
| Fannie has three older daughters. | |
| Dewey Goodman (age 42) | 1946 |

## HINKCES

| | |
|---|---|
| Sam (father) | 1875-1943, (died at age 68) |
| Lucille (mother) | 1875-1963, (died at 88) |
| Violet (age 92) | 1895-1987 |

Daisy (age 88) 1901-1987
Zachary 1904-1920
Rose & Zachary were twins.
Rose (age 83) 1904-1987
Lily (age 65) 1923- Married, with children

## JACKSON

Etta Mae (age 74) 1914-
Ben 1913-Died in the 50's

## MAAS

Elsa (age 96) 1892-
Thomas (son) (age 67) 1921-

## MILLER (Rev)

Cyrus (age 68) 1920
Nell (age 63) 1925
Married in 1948 for 40 years

## MOONEY

Clive (age 62) 1926
Calvin (father)

## SCHOEN

Albert (age 65) 1923

Amy Bronson Schoen 1923-1953
Twins 1947-1952

John (brother to Albert) 1925
Martha (Wife)(age 62) 1926
Julian (age 11) grandson
Isabella (age 7½) granddaughter

## WEBSTER

| | |
|---|---|
| Selma (72) | 1916 |
| Marla (daughter) (35) | 1953 |

Marla has 3 small girls: Katy, 6; Maddy, 4; Lizzy, 3

Printed in the United States
26215LVS00001B/377

9 781595 070654